DAY OF THE DEAD

A GIA SANTELLA CRIME THRILLER
BOOK 5

KRISTI BELCAMINO

LIQUID MIND PUBLISHING

Liquid Mind Publishing
*This is a work of fiction. All characters, names, places and events are the product of the
author's imagination or used fictitiously.*

For my awesome readers. Thank you for reading my books!

GIA SANTELLA CRIME THRILLER SERIES

Enjoying the Gia Santella series? Scan below to order more books today!

Vendetta

Vigilante

Vengeance

Black Widow

Day of the Dead

Border Line

Night Fall

Stone Cold

Cold as Death

Cold Blooded

Dark Shadows

Dark Vengeance

Dark Justice

Deadly Justice

Deadly Lies

PROLOGUE

San Francisco, California

Present Day

Women with skull faces and black rose bouquets in their arms brushed against me.

The Grim Reaper was headed my way, his deep-set eyes, poking out of a black hood, bored into me. He walked jerkily forward, his stark, white face expressionless, unsmiling, unnerving.

It was like a game of chicken. Except that he was going the wrong way in the procession. The people between us scattered, some scowling or swearing. He outweighed me by 100 pounds and towered over me by at least a foot, but this was one asshole who wasn't going to intimidate me. I held steady, meeting his eyes without blinking. I lifted my chin in challenge.

The distance closed between us. He never took his eyes off me. As he grew closer, I scanned his hands. They hung by his side. Empty. No gleaming flash of gunmetal or silver.

But as the distance closed between us and he didn't veer

from my direction nor avert his gaze from mine, I reached behind me, back into my waistband.

Without taking my eyes off of his, I swiftly withdrew my dagger and tucked the hand holding the blade into the folds of my long skirt. His eyes flickered and widened. He'd seen.

We were mere feet away. At the last minute, when I could smell his sweat emanating from beneath the thick, black robe, he swore and swerved, mumbling something about "crazy motherfucker."

"You have no idea," I said over my shoulder.

Relief flooded my body.

I wouldn't have to fight for my life just yet. Soon, though.

Barely turning my head, I scanned the crowd. Most of the women had face paint, and like me, were dressed as *La Calvera Catrina's*—the elegant patron of the Day of the Dead. I wore a deep red, satin ball gown that billowed out around me and a black lace shawl. My white-painted face also featured beautiful pink roses trailing across my temple, and my black-rimmed eyes were bordered with delicate turquoise and lavender flowers. Many of the men wore silky black tuxedos with red bow ties. But their white faces were sinister and frightening. No matter how they were dressed, the paradegoers shuffled or lurched or limped as we made our way to the Festival of Altars at Garfield Square. After all, we were supposed to be dead.

It had been my idea to meet at the park. Do the exchange in a public place. It gave me a fighting chance. At least that's what I told myself. They knew I was coming. However, I wouldn't take the obvious route to the meeting point. I would arrive my own way, disguised in my own *Dia de los Muertos* costume and hopefully blend into the procession, indistinguishable from anyone else.

Did he hope that my murder would go unnoticed because of the crowd?

Because that's what he had in mind—my murder.

He hadn't fooled me for a second. He wanted to meet me to kill me.

Maybe the Grim Reaper hadn't tried to kill me just now, but someone else was waiting in the shadows to do so. It was just a matter of time. Every face and body marching down Treat Street was suspect.

Suddenly, the park was before us.

It glowed from the street. Thousands of candles filled the park, illuminating colorful altars—*ofrendas*.

I made my way through the altars, passing a row over from the one I had left for Bobby. My eyes flicked as I passed, and my heart clenched.

Bobby, I'm sorry. For everything. I love you.

My fist closed tightly around my dagger. The reassuring weight of the gun in my ankle holster and the other blade strapped tightly to my left thigh gave me a false confidence.

I was already outnumbered.

As soon as I stepped away from the lights of the altars into the far recesses of the park, all sound receded as well—the laughter, prayers, and Aztec drumming drowned out by the thudding of my heart in my ears.

I stepped around a tree. I sensed them before I saw them.

I squinted in the dark, trying to make out the shapes before me. Then I saw him. His face was painted white and marked up like a skull. Perfect. It suited him.

"It's over, Gia. It's time to come with me."

His words sent a lightning bolt of fear down my spine.

"Where is he?" My voice was shrill. I couldn't hide my panic.

I swiveled my head to make sure nobody was creeping up behind me before I searched the cluster of figures for his familiar form. As my eyes adjusted slightly, I saw two figures holding up a third slumped body.

Relief soared through me. James. He was alive.

In that split second, they attacked in a blur of arms and legs, fists and kicks and punches.

I managed to land a blow to a kidney and heard a satisfying whoosh of air, then threw a hand blade to someone's cloaked neck, but still the pummeling continued. A particularly well-aimed blow to my cheek sent me reeling and scrambling to keep my balance as the long folds of my skirt got caught up in my legs. I came back with a wide swinging arc of one leg that succeeded when my boot slammed with a man's chest. But the damn skirt was a liability. I had known that earlier tonight, but the need for a disguise had won out.

Another blow took me off guard enough for someone to wrap an arm around my neck. I flailed about for my dagger, but it had shot out of my hand earlier. I allowed myself to fall completely limp, causing both me and my attacker to fall to the ground where I flipped the voluminous skirt of my dress up and over our heads as I repeatedly slammed the back of my skull into the man's nose until he finally released me.

I tried to crab walk out of danger, but another large figure slammed a heavy boot down, nearly missing my gut and stomping on my dress, pinning me to the dirt.

I was losing.

I couldn't see a way out on my own. One man was leaning against a tree moaning. But that still left two others for me to fight off. Luckily, they hadn't been able to come at me at the same time yet since one of them was holding James.

But then, with some luck, I was able to land a solid kick between the guy's eyes, and he stumbled backward for a few feet before he collapsed.

That left the guy holding James.

He pushed James back onto the ground and charged. He slammed me into a tree trunk. I gasped. Excruciating pain exploded in my side. I was certain my ribs were broken and wanted to curl up and die, but there was a heavy boot headed my way. I ducked. Tree bark rained down into my hair.

Across the park, the *Dia de los Muertos* festivities continued with the throb of bone-thumping drums as the Aztec dancers performed in massive headdresses. From further away, the strains of Mariachi music also helped to drown out the grunts and muffled exclamations from our melee.

That's when I noticed that James had stood and was coming closer, walking unsteadily. I needed his help. The pain in my side was nearly unbearable. I fell to the ground, knowing I was in a vulnerable position, but it was the only way I could reach down to my ankle holster and free my handgun.

"James!" I shouted and tossed the gun. I watched him catch it just as my attacker slammed my head into the tree trunk.

At first, I thought I was truly seeing stars from the head blow, but then I realized in my stunned state that it was a flashlight blinding me. Voices broke the silence.

James whirled. The gun in his hand caught the light.

"Police! Drop the gun! Drop the gun! Drop the gun!"

Everything happened at once.

"He's a cop," I screamed.

"San Francisco PD," James shouted.

But our words couldn't compete with the deafening blast of the gun.

The world went silent. Then returned full force with the echo of my scream ricocheting in my head as I frantically crawled, clawing at the dirt with my fingernails, toward where James lay flat on his back on the ground.

1

BEFORE ...

"Your mama doesn't like me because I'm white."

I said the words around the cigarette dangling from my lips.

James rolled his eyes—at my words and at the cigarette. "I thought you quit." He kicked at a leaf on the sidewalk between us and shook his head.

I used a match to light the cigarette and flicked it into the wide, round driveway of the hotel, knowing this gesture would annoy him even more. I didn't usually litter, but I was pissed off. And besides, I knew the driveway was swept like every hour here, so the fancy-ass guests didn't have to step foot on anything dirty when they got out of their Rolls Royces and Benzes.

My smoking was a sore point with us. James was a fervent anti-smoker, and ever since I'd started seeing him again, I'd been hiding my bad habit. But I was about to blow and needed nicotine to tamp down my emotions before I said something I'd regret.

I snapped my silver cigarette case closed and tucked it into my bag.

"I needed a smoke after being in there." I gestured with the lit cherry of the cigarette toward the windows of the hotel restaurant. From our vantage point, we could see the ambient lighting of the fancy restaurant and the white table clothes and black silk seat covers.

At one table in the back, sat James's elegant mother and aunt. Both women wore Chanel suits with delicate kitten-heeled pumps and perfectly coiffed hair and makeup.

And then there was me.

I'd dressed up. But my idea of fancy clothes was a little different. I'd worn my Jimmy Choo stilettos—black patent T-straps with the signature red soles—some nice black slacks, and a red silk blouse that I usually wore open down to my sternum. But tonight, to be respectful, I'd buttoned it up, so it only gave a brief glimpse of my collarbone.

Even so, I felt like a freaking streetwalker sitting next to them. It was also how they looked at me—like something the cat dragged in.

After dessert, I'd excused myself while the women "lingered over a coffee" so I could go smoke and feel sorry for myself. The dinner had been awkward. The two women had exchanged pointed looks when I said "Dammit."

If they only knew how hard I'd been trying not to let the F-bomb fly.

Hanging out with his mother and aunt in a chichi hotel restaurant wasn't exactly how I wanted to spend my evening with James. I'd rather eat take-out in bed after we'd gotten busy. Because he looked particularly yummy tonight. He'd worn a navy dress shirt and tight black jeans with Italian shoes. The shirt clung to his toned chest, and I have to admit that a few times during dinner I'd fantasized about ripping the buttons open with my teeth later in the evening. Now my gaze was level with his lips, and maybe it was the bottle of red wine, but I was slightly mesmerized by how they moved when he spoke.

"Are you trying to say meeting my mother and aunt makes you need a cigarette," James said. His jaw was set firm.

Why had he followed me out here anyway? I'd wanted to be alone to pout and feel sorry for myself. Anger flared through me. Why had I even been thinking about sex or a future with James? Why bother? His mother hated me. I could tell. That wasn't exactly the best recipe for foreplay.

"You heard me," I took another deep drag and exhaled.

He frowned.

"Your mama and auntie don't like me. Why? Because I didn't go to an Ivy League college?"

Like your last girlfriend.

"Because I'm white?"

Not like your last girlfriend.

"Because I smoke? Because we fuck, and we're not married? Or all of the above."

He shrugged. "They like you."

I shook my head, my long dark hair swinging. "Don't start lying to me now."

He exhaled and then surprised the shit out of me by reaching over and taking my Dunhill out of my hand. I stared in astonishment as he took the cigarette, rimmed with my bright red lipstick, and put it between his lips. He inhaled, handed it back to me and then exhaled.

My mouth was open, and for once I was speechless. I was even more shocked that he didn't choke and had blown the smoke out expertly. I narrowed my eyes in suspicion as he spoke. I guess I wasn't the only one who kept secrets in this relationship.

"It's not that they don't like you," he began.

I waited, lifting an eyebrow.

"It's that they don't want to see me get hurt."

I closed my eyes.

That was worse than them not liking me. I couldn't guarantee I wouldn't hurt James. I'd stopped seeing him once before worried about that very thing. I opened my mouth to respond but sat there gaping like a fish out of water.

I had nothing.

His face closed off to me as he turned on one heel and left.

I was about to chase after him when a livery car pulled up and the window rolled down.

"Gia?"

It was Darling. One of my closest friends.

I started toward James' retreating figure, but hesitated. What was she doing here?

"Do you have a second? I hate to bother you on your date, but this is important."

I gave one last glance toward the hotel door before I turned back to Darling.

"Sure, what's up?"

2

I TEXTED JAMES FROM THE BACK OF THE CAR SPEEDING TOWARD the hospital.

That's why I was no good for James. No wonder his mother and aunt disliked me. They saw right through me. I was a nightmare in a relationship.

I quickly dictated my text.

"Please apologize to your mother and aunt. Darling showed up, and we are on our way to the hospital. A girl she knows is in trouble, and they need my help."

I hit send and held my breath. I watched the little dots that showed he was typing.

I quickly dictated. "And I'm sorry."

"What am I supposed to tell my mother?" He wrote back.

"I swear it's an emergency. I'll meet you guys at the theater." I glanced at Darling and then dictated more. "It shouldn't take that long."

I wanted to write that his mother and aunt were surely ecstatic to spend a few hours alone with him, aka—without me, but I restrained myself.

Because Darling had said one thing that made me get in that car and forget about everything else.

"I think the Albino's back."

Kraig King was the national head of the country's largest white supremacist group. He'd taken over our neighborhood once, preying on the homeless. He'd taken the downtrodden, the most down-and-out of all of us, and murdered them, stuffing their bodies in massive vats of acid to dissolve. Until I'd exposed him, and he'd fled. I'd regretted letting him escape alive ever since.

And he was the one who'd marked me.

I fingered the scar that ran from my temple down my cheek. It had grown strangely hot at Darling's words. I thought of Harry Potter and gave a strangled cackling laugh. My scar couldn't possibly *really* be hot. This wasn't a goddamn story in a book.

This wasn't a magical world. This was fucking San Francisco in the twenty-first century, and King was a man who could—and would if I had anything to do with it—die like any other man.

There was nothing make-believe about the pure, inherent evil of King.

And now he was apparently back.

I wasn't surprised that Darling was the first to know of his return.

Darling was the unofficial Empress of the Tenderloin, and as a result, everybody came to her for help. Tonight, she'd received a call from a friend of hers. The woman's daughter had been missing for the past two months. She'd grown angry one day and run away. The girl had become addicted to prescription painkillers and they'd fought over the girl's drug use. She'd been caught stealing a bottle of the medication from her grandmother's medicine cabinet.

The woman had reported it to the police, but, as often happens, as soon as they heard the girl was addicted to opiates, they wrote her off as a runaway instead of hunting for her like a missing person.

Meanwhile, the woman had been sick-to-death with worry. Nobody on the streets had any idea where the girl had gone. Every time the phone rang, the mother expected it to be the police telling her they'd found her daughter overdosed in an alley.

Then, weeks after her daughter had slammed the door and ran out of the house, the woman got a strange phone call. The voice on the line sounded like that of a female teenager. She said the missing girl/daughter was holed up in a house on Tompkins Avenue in Bernal Heights.

The address belonged to a rehab facility—a private house where young people hooked on opiates received treatment.

The mother was overjoyed. Not only was her daughter alive, but she was finally getting help with her addiction.

But when she showed up at the facility and asked to see Layla Boudreau, the receptionist told her they didn't have any patients by that name. And when the mother described her daughter and showed a picture, the receptionist shook her head.

There was nobody there by that name or description.

Baffled, the mother left.

In disbelief, the mother hid in her car and watched the comings and goings of the house for a few days but never saw anything except the receptionist come and go for her shift and twice a day a large black car entered an attached garage. The garage door always closed before the mother could see how many people were in the car.

The mother gave up on finding her daughter and spent her days drinking her grief away. Until tonight.

Tonight, she'd gotten another call.

This caller, who again sounded like a young girl, said her daughter was at the hospital.

The woman raced to the hospital and found her daughter in ICU. In a coma. She'd overdosed. Nobody could say where she had come from or what had happened.

Finally, she found out that an orderly had seen a black car pull up to the ER entrance. Two people had leaped out of the front seat, carrying a body. They'd dropped the girl onto the ground before speeding off.

The orderly, who had been smoking in the shadows, said she saw a man with a shock of white hair sitting in the back seat.

The woman had called Darling who had immediately set off to pick Gia up on her way to the hospital.

"You think it might be him. The Albino?" Darling asked, fixing her lipstick and peering into her compact mirror at her massive kohl-rimmed eyes as they grew closer to the hospital. Her lioness mane of dark curls bobbed as she spoke, along with her ample bosom.

"It sure sounds like King," I said. My stomach was flip-flopping, and it wasn't because of the prime rib and red wine from dinner.

"That's what I thought too," Darling said. "That's why I came straight to you."

"Thanks, Darling. But why would he be back? Would he be that brazen? He must know he's still a wanted man around here."

"Hiding in plain sight works for some," Darling said, pressing her lips together to blot her lipstick.

"You're right," I said. "But what's his game now?"

"Kids. On drugs," Darling said. "More than one."

I leaned forward.

"I have two other mothers who say their girls vanished without a trace the same way. Both hooked on opiates. Both ran away, and there's no word from my contacts on the streets. I'd bet my last dime, King got his hooks into them girls too."

I thought about it. "He doesn't play small time. What's his game? And what's up with that rehab place? It's got to be a front for something. But what?"

My mind was racing with possibilities, each more sinister than the last.

Darling smiled and patted my knee. "That's what you're going to find out."

3

When we arrived at the ICU, Darling spoke in hushed tones to the nurse who nodded and then disappeared down the hall. We waited in the cold, sterile hall. The only sound was the beeping and buzzing of different machines emanating from open doors. All the doors in ICU were open, but curtains hung between the hall and the patients in their beds. At the end of the hall was a waiting room with large orange couches and vending machines. One family sat huddled together, red-eyed and crying. An elderly man sat alone in a chair across from them, his lower lip trembling.

This was not a cheerful place. This was a place where people waited to hear the fate of their loved ones, and it probably could go either way.

The nurse came back and said something to Darling in a low voice. My friend turned to me. "We can go back now."

I followed Darling's broad back down the hall until the nurse stood before one doorway.

Darling nodded at the nurse, and we entered the room. We stepped through the curtain. I wasn't prepared for what I saw.

A young, slim girl barely took up any room in the bed. Wires and tubes led from her mouth and arms to massive machines surrounding her bed. The room was filled with the sounds of beeping and the rhythmic whoosh of an artificial respirator.

The girl was so small. Long, dark lashes rested on her pale white cheeks. But other than that, I couldn't distinguish any of her features. Her small face was overtaken by machinery and tubes.

A pink-painted toenail poked out from the bottom of the sheet that stretched only to her ankles. A woman with deep circles beneath her eyes sat in a chair at the edge of the bed, rubbing the girl's feet with hands dappled with age spots. I assumed it was the girl's mother.

The woman had deep circles under her eyes. Her brown hair showed two inches of gray roots. She'd slapped some pink lipstick on, but it had smeared outside her lips. This woman looked like she had been to hell and back.

Looking up as we took in the heartbreaking scene, the woman said, "They said I could do this. Keep the circulation going you know. And maybe she can feel it."

A lump rose in my throat and the desire to run out of there as fast as I could overcame me, but I managed to choke down both the lump and the urge to bail. I needed to keep my shit together. There was nothing I could do for this girl, but maybe I could stop this from happening to anyone else.

"At first, they thought it was an overdose," the mother said, "because of the needle they found in her arm and all that. But then they said there's something else. Some poison or something in her bloodwork. Like maybe the stuff was tainted. It don't look good. They said maybe she won't make it, and even if she does she won't be my same girl. She's my baby. The only one still at home. My sweetest girl."

I couldn't take anymore. That girl was going to die. Or worse. I felt like I was going to throw up.

"Ma'am," I said, speaking for the first time. "Can you give me the address of that house on Tompkins Avenue?"

She recited it to me. I didn't write it down. It was engraved on my memory already.

"I'll be in touch."

Darling gave me a startled look as I turned and left.

As soon as I was outside the ICU unit, I leaned against the wall and closed my eyes trying to catch my breath. I clenched my fists repeatedly to the rhythm of my pounding heart.

If that girl died, it was all on me.

Because if King was on the loose and had caused this to happen to that little girl, it was entirely and utterly my fault.

I was the one who'd let him go the first time.

Right then and there, I vowed that if he was in town, I'd hunt him down and stop him from ever hurting another person again if it was the last thing I ever did.

Seeing that little girl had guaranteed I had no other choice.

I'd die before I let King hurt another innocent child again.

4

OPENING MY EYES, I NOTICED THE ICU NURSE QUICKLY LOOK AWAY. I'm sure she'd seen much worse on this floor than me struggling to hold it together.

I blinked and that's when I saw movement.

In a dark corner, was an empty room. But two seconds ago, I saw a girl in the darkness of the doorway. From where the girl was, the nurse couldn't see her, but the girl could clearly see the entrance to Layla's room.

When she saw me looking, she shrank deeper into the shadows. I winked at her.

A beeping noise from the nurse's station made me jump. The girl jumped too. But the sounds weren't coming from Layla's room. The nurse stood and disappeared into another room across the hall.

I slipped into the room and took the girl's arm somewhat forcefully.

"Let's talk."

She scratched at my grip and sputtered, but I yanked her out into the light just as the nurse returned and gave us a look.

"Come on, sweetie. Let's go grab a bite to eat and then we'll come back." I smiled at the nurse.

The girl scowled but didn't resist as I led her out the doors of the ICU.

Once the automatic doors slammed shut, she yanked her arm away. "Crazy bitch."

I laughed. "Have we met?"

Her frown deepened. I took her in. She was petite and wiry with brightly dyed red hair and dark roots. Her eyes were huge pools of sea green, and her face was scarred with acne. She scratched her bare arms, and I knew then she was an addict.

"I don't want to leave her," she said, trying to push past me back into the ICU.

My smile faded, and I nodded. "I know. Let's get you some food and then we'll come back."

Her face crumpled. "What if she dies? I can't go get food. I can't be gone. What if something happens? I need to be there."

She drew back as two chatting men in scrubs passed and turned down the hall. I heard the sound of coins and realized there was a vending machine nearby.

"Why are you hiding?"

She shrugged. "I don't know Layla's mama."

I nodded.

"I won't force you to go to the cafeteria. I'm only going to take a minute of your time and then you can go back in there. I promise. I'll even introduce you to my friend. She knows Layla's mom. She'll make sure you're welcome in the room."

I hoped I was telling the truth.

She wiped a tear away.

"How did you know Layla was here?"

"I'm the one called her mama."

I examined her. Her lower lip trembled. She was struggling valiantly not to cry. Tough kid. "You may have saved her life."

Her face crumbled and her entire body shook, but no tears came out.

I squinted at her. "When's the last time you ate or drank?"

She shrugged. "I don't know."

Her face and clothing were filthy.

"Are you living on the streets?" It was a rhetorical question. "Listen. Were you with Layla when this happened?"

She looked away, but nodded.

My heartbeat quickened. "In that house?"

Another tiny nod. Then, "I seen them take Layla. She looked half dead. They were all freaking out. They forgot to lock the main door. I ran out. I grabbed the lady's wallet and ran."

"What lady? What wallet?"

"I threw it away after I got the money out." She crossed her arms and glared at me. "You gonna call the cops?"

I scoffed. "Hardly."

Her eyes never left the doors to ICU.

I gestured toward the vending machines. "Come on. Let's get you something to eat and drink and then I'll introduce you to my friend."

Armed with crackers and chips and candy bars and three waters, I led her back to the ICU. I poked my head in.

"Darling? Can I talk to you for a sec in the hall?"

"Mmmhhhmm."

To her credit, Darling barely looked at the girl.

"What's up, Gia?"

"This young lady—hey, what's your name?"

"Josie." Her voice was small.

I went on. "Well, anyway, Josie called Layla's mother. And she's been hiding out over there in the dark in that empty room."

"You must be worried sick," Darling said. "Why don't you come sit with us, but I warn you, it's tough to see Layla. You okay with that?"

The girl nodded.

"Wait here," I said to the girl and took Darling's arm. I walked to the end of the hall. "Can you keep an eye on her? Don't let her leave. I think she might know what's going on at that house."

"Sure thing."

I turned to leave.

"Where you going again?" Darling asked.

I sighed. "I'm trying to salvage my relationship with James and his mother. And then I'll be back. Might be late, though. I've got to see a play. Snore."

Darling laughed. "Oh, have fun. Tell James thank you for letting me steal you away." Then she sobered. "He's back, Gia. I just know it."

I knew it too.

I'd barely set foot out of the hospital and was waiting for a livery car near a bus stop bench when Darling called.

"She's gone."

"What? I told you to keep an eye on her." I said. I was disappointed but knew that keeping an eye on a scrappy homeless girl wasn't her job.

"Layla. Layla's gone." Her voice was leaden.

"Oh no." I sunk onto the bus stop bench.

"And that girl's gone, too," Darling said. "She slipped out amid the chaos of alarms going off, doctor and nurses running in, and Layla's poor mama weeping and wailing."

"I'm so sorry." My eyes stayed locked on the front door of the hospital as I spoke. I needed to find Josie. She was my key to finding out about King and whether he was connected to that rehab house. But then I realized a girl that street smart wouldn't leave out the front door.

I hung up and watched the front door for sixty seconds, giving the girl time to ride the elevator down, and when I didn't see anything, I took off at a run. I circled the building looking for other exits. Besides the Emergency entrance, there were several other doors at loading docks and one door for employees to exit for breaks.

A man was smoking a cigarette outside.

"Excuse me?" I said. "Have you seen a teenage girl."

"Scrawny little redhead that needs a bath?"

"Yep."

"She took off that way." He gestured to the adjacent road. "Hopped on the number four."

The bus stop sign was nearly hidden behind a tree.

I sighed.

"Thank you. Have a good night."

Out front again, I waited for the car I'd ordered to arrive.

When the sedan pulled up, I got in and spoke while still staring at my phone. "Hey there. We're going to do a little scavenger hunt. Following bus four's route."

"I don't know that route." The man spoke with a slight accent. He had silver-rimmed glasses that reflected the street lights.

"I got you covered. Just drive south."

We made it to the next closest bus stop. Empty. And the second. The third was a transfer station. If she got off there there's no way I'd know. It was packed with bodies. We waited for a few seconds as I scanned the crowd and made sure she wasn't in it

By the time we got to the fourth stop, the bus had just pulled away. I scanned the streets around us. I didn't see anyone.

"You're doing great," I told the driver. "Pull up beside the bus so I can see who's onboard."

He did so at a stop light.

I scanned the heads. I didn't see her.

The transfer station. Dammit.

I wanted to punch the back of the seat, but instead I just gave the driver my home address.

At home, I peeled off my clothes and crawled into bed in my underwear, exhausted. Django curled up beside me. I nuzzled my face into his fur and scratched under his chin. I was drifting asleep when I sat up straight in bed.

"Fuck me!"

So much for meeting up with James and his mother.

5

IN OUR ROUGH AND TUMBLE NEIGHBORHOOD, WHICH WE RESIDENTS affectionately called the T.L., short for the Tenderloin, people who didn't trust authorities—usually for good reason—turned to Darling for help.

If she were Italian, like me, I would have said she was the Godmother. But with her regal Cleopatra bearing, the "empress" title fit her well. She was about six feet tall and double my weight, and she moved with the feline grace of a panther. Her preternatural huge black eyes were always rimmed with thick kohl like Cleopatra's. She didn't put up with any shit, although I'd never heard her raise her voice to anyone. Usually you knew you were in trouble if her voice lowered to nearly a whisper.

She was my best female friend. But she was really more like a surrogate mother to me.

When there were gang disputes, Darling mediated. When a man treated a woman badly, she made sure that man knew his time on earth was limited if he continued his behavior. When rich developers tried to bully some of the old mom-and-pop businesses in the T.L. into selling, Darling made sure they slunk out of town with their tail between their legs.

She was a badass. And she was rich as sin. I thought I was pretty well off, but I think Darling outdid me. She owned three houses and I saw something once that showed she had stashed gobs of money in offshore accounts.

"I don't touch any of that," she'd said. "That's my emergency escape money. If this country goes south, I'm out of here."

Her most profitable business was providing top-notch, foolproof documents for people who needed new identities. Her biggest clients were abused women escaping dangerous situations. She refused to work with criminals, though.

The back office of her salon served as her headquarters. It was outfitted like a cozy living room in a mansion with a TV that took up one entire wall and a grouping of white leather couches. That's where I picked her up.

I'd wanted to arrive at the rehab house the second the sun rose over the mountains in the East Bay, but Darling had other plans.

She was busy all day helping Layla's mother with the funeral arrangements.

I'd spent the morning feeling sorry for myself. I called James, but he wouldn't pick up. So, I texted him: "I'm a total asshole."

Nothing.

"I'm sorry. Will you give me a chance to explain?"

Nothing.

Finally, around two, I headed to train at the Dojo.

I needed to work off some of my anxiety.

Now, showered and somewhat calmer, I was at Darling's salon. I knocked and made faces at the security cameras above the steel-reinforced door until the door buzzed open

Darling posed in front of the mirror fluffing her hair. She had on a green silk blouse and—I did a double take—a heavy choke necklace thick with jade. Her humongous black eyes were lined in her signature Cleopatra style. She looked great. Over-dressed for the Oscars, maybe, but great.

"It's not a beauty contest," I said. "In fact, I'll bet you a bottle of Veuve Clicquot that there won't even be a red carpet."

She rolled her striking eyes at me and reached for a small clutch.

"Gia, you never know when you might end up immortalized in a photograph while you are out in this city."

I yawned. I'd heard that song and dance from her before.

"I think I'm just gonna start calling you the Queen of Sheba. Maybe Sheeb for short?"

She ignored me.

"Daughter of Isis?"

Again, she pretended not to hear me.

"I know," I said, snapping. "How about just plain Cleopatra?"

"Are you done?" She raised a perfect eyebrow, and I couldn't help but laugh. As hard as I tried I could never out-sass Darling. She chalked up a win every time without even trying.

As we walked out, I glanced in the mirror. When I got ready after my shower, I hadn't been worried about a fucking photo op. I'd slashed on some red lipstick so at least it didn't look like I'd just woken up, but the rest of my face was bare of makeup. My hair wasn't too tangled, considering I hadn't combed it from the shower. At least it was clean. It hung down my back, blending into the rest of my dark outfit. I nodded in approval of my own choice of faded black jeans, motorcycle boots, and black T-shirt. They meant I was ready to kick ass if things went south.

When we got out to the sidewalk, Darling drew up short in front of my car.

She planted her feet and crossed her arms across her bountiful chest.

I gave her a quizzical glance as I hit the button turning off the car alarm.

"I'm not getting into that." She pointed a purple manicured nail at my black Ferrari.

I realized it was the first time I'd driven us anywhere. Normally, Darling picked me up. She relied on a regular car service and always sat in the back of big black town cars like the royalty she was.

Grabbing the handle, I opened the passenger side door. "It'll be fun."

"Nuh uh." But she walked over.

I felt a little guilty as she huffed and puffed getting inside. It wasn't the easiest car to get in and out of, I'll admit. Once she was settled in, I said, "Buckle up, baby," and closed the door.

A few minutes later we were zipping up the windy road toward Bernal Heights.

"Whew!" Darling said, making sure her seatbelt was tight. "This thing's got some get up and go."

I smiled but kept my eyes on the road. It was narrow and tricky, and I didn't want to take out the row of cars that lined it.

As we crawled higher above the city, the road narrowed with even more cars parked tight on both sides of the street. We passed the address twice before I finally found a spot to park as another car pulled out of a spot a few houses down.

The house itself was typical of the neighborhood—a one-story, long and low, with a big front window.

As we walked up the front steps that window revealed a homey interior—a plush couch, end tables, a chair and a large reception desk.

The woman behind the desk seemed to sense us and looked up sharply.

At first glance, she was the spitting image of Daenerys Targaryen from the *Game of Thrones* show. She had ice-blonde hair, mostly pulled back and falling down her back except for a few ringlets that hung by her cheekbones. She even wore a

Greek goddess-style dress like the actress did. A white number.

But as I drew closer, I saw that this woman was probably twenty years older than the actress who played the Mother of Dragons on the show. Her neck showed deep lines as she turned toward someone else and said something. Then her head pivoted back, her eyes boring into me. I examined her openly. Her face was ultra-smooth and tight. Some good plastic surgery for sure.

"What's up with blondie?" Darling said.

"Good question."

The door swung open at the same time we knocked. She stood in the doorway, one hand on the doorknob, her head cocked, seemingly waiting for us to speak.

"Good afternoon."

I sagged in relief. Darling was handling it.

"May I help you?" She had a Russian accent. Up close, I saw I was right. She had about thirty years on the Dragon Mother Stormborn actress.

"I believe a friend of mine is staying here."

I practically scoffed at the way Darling phrased it. Like it was a god damn resort on the Riviera.

Stormborn didn't budge.

But that didn't stop Darling who hefted herself up the last step and barged her way through, forcing the Mother of Dragons out of the way.

I smiled and followed my friend.

The woman hesitated long enough in the doorway to let us know she was annoyed and then she let the door slam behind her. She briskly walked past us and slid into a chair behind her desk.

"I'll notify the doctor," she said as she lifted the receiver of a phone and tapped in a number.

Darling and I both stayed standing in front of her desk.

There was only one interior door, and it was to the right. It had a small window cut into it like you'd see at a police station. And it looked heavy. It had a thick deadbolt lock.

"Two women are here asking to see a guest."

A guest, my ass.

Keeping her eyes on me, the woman nodded, pursed her lips together, and said, "Yes, doctor."

I scanned the wall behind her. Most doctor's offices had the doctor's medical degree or other credentials framed. I turned to Darling and said in a low voice. "Let's ask to see medical degrees, all that kind of shit."

Darling didn't look at me but nodded.

Stormborn hung up the phone with a smug look.

"I'm sorry you'll have to make an appointment to speak to the doctor about visiting privileges. He's caught up in something urgent at this moment."

"That's odd," I said. "Is it difficult to get these so-called 'visiting privileges?' I'd think if we knew one of your *guests*, we should be able to just come visit, right? Without an appointment."

She smiled a saccharine grin. "We have a bit of an unconventional way of doing things," she said. "We are exceedingly strict about visits from outsiders. It is what makes us special. We sometimes do things differently, and that is why we are so successful. Dr. Moore is considered a bit of a rebel in the medical community."

Her speech sounded stilted, but then I remembered that slight Russian accent. English must be her second language. I frowned at her words, though. Why was she proud of this and volunteering this information? Didn't she know that one of her "guests" died last night? And yet she kept yapping.

"Dr. Moore believes the only way to effectively cure someone of opioid addiction is to completely isolate them from their previous lives and who they knew."

"For how long?" Darling asked, folding her arms over her chest and cocking her head while watching the other woman.

"As long as it takes."

"How long does that take, say, on average?" I asked, winking at Darling.

Dragon Lady ignored me and kept unspooling her rehearsed spiel.

"It's a proven method to cure the addiction. He's saved hundreds of lives. He's going to be famous one day." She beamed with pride. Why was she so proud? It wasn't like her mug was going to be on the cover besides Dr. Killjoys. Unless maybe they were a thing?

"When can we get that appointment?" I said.

The woman looked down at something on her desk and frowned. "Unfortunately, Dr. Moore is going to be out of the country, starting tomorrow, for maybe a month."

"Of course, he is." I shot a sarcastic smile at her. "So, put us down for a month from today."

Darling raised an eyebrow at me.

"We'll be here," I said.

Darling paced the waiting room, clucking to herself and admiring the art—giant photographs of the Golden Gate bridge at Sunset and the Bay Bridge at night. A small can of paint sat on the floor behind a potted plant. She jutted her chin at it so I would see it.

"How long you been here?" I asked the blonde.

Again, the Mother of Dragons did a good job of not answering me. She should run for office or something.

"This is our newest facility. We recently received a generous donation from an investor that has allowed us to expand our reach. We now have two facilities."

I eyed the locked door. "You lock them up? Your *guests*." Again, I drew out the word.

The woman gave me a patronizing look. "You obviously haven't spent much time around addicts, have you?"

I bit back my retort and turned away. Darling stepped up to the desk and leaned over it, getting right in Stormborn's personal space.

"Do you have a business license I could examine?" she batted her Cleopatra eyes innocently. God love the woman.

Dragon Lady frowned and tapped her lip with a fingernail.

"Hmm," she stalled. "I'd have to ask the doctor where it is. We are still in the process of unpacking. As I said, we are new here."

"How about a framed medical degree?" I said. "Most doctors hang that before the paint is even dry."

"I'll ask." Her voice was tight.

Darling took my arm and steered me toward the door as she said, "Thank you. We'll be back in a month."

We headed back to Darling's salon, and I parked my Ferrari out front. Instead of going inside, we walked to Katrina's for dinner.

The restaurant was bustling, and we hunched in the lobby with others waiting for a table. But Katrina must've been told we were there because a hostess met my eye and gestured for us to follow. She led us along the black marble floors, past the wall of candles and oversized mirrors covering two of the four walls of the main room, and drew back the velvet curtains to reveal my blue velvet booth with the engraved metal plate that said "Gia Santella."

Within seconds Katrina was at our table.

When I first met Katrina, she was working as a bartender. I'd helped finance Café Katrina because of my gut instinct. I'd been right. The place was now world famous.

No matter how long I knew her, I was always floored by Katrina's ethereal Asian beauty. Porcelain skin, blue eyes, and a Playboy cover girl's body. She could've been a movie star or top model, but she was a smart, tough-as-nails business owner.

She air-kissed our cheeks and then slid into the booth with us. She handed our menus to a passing waiter.

"I've already put your order in."

Darling harrumphed.

Katrina laughed. "Don't worry. I made sure Leonardo includes your au gratin potatoes."

Darling made a grumpy face. "Good thing."

"Italian?" I asked.

"No. I'm having him make some Asian fusion for you."

"No I mean Leonardo?"

Katrina shook her head as the waiter brought some raw sashimi slices of yellowtail tuna.

"Persian."

"Okay then. So *almost* as good looking and talented as the Italians," I said, looking away to hide my smart-ass grin.

"How's James?" Katrina asked.

I eagerly reached for my glass and didn't come up for air again until it was gone I ordered another.

Katrina and Darling exchanged a look that I ignored. They weren't the ones whose boyfriend wouldn't even answer his phone. I'd tried again on the drive back to the salon.

"Is there a problem?" Katrina wouldn't let it go, homing in on my troubles like a heat-seeking missile.

Darling's hush was loud enough for me to hear. I poured another drink and downed it before answering.

"It's Darling's fault."

Darling scoffed and downed her own drink. Katrina's eyes were like laser beams.

I softened. "Well, not really."

After I explained what happened, Katrina shook her head. "He's not very understanding, is he?"

"Katrina! I ditched him and his mother and aunt at a restaurant without saying goodbye, and then I flaked on meeting him."

"Oh my God," Darling said. "Are you defending him now?"

"Maybe." My voice was meek.

"He should know that you'd only do that unless it were absolutely necessary," Katrina said, standing as three waiters brought our food. "I mean, you would never be inconsiderate like that unless it was important. Life-or-death, right?"

I nodded.

"Mmmhhhmm," Darling said, nodding, her big black eyes flashing.

A waiter put a plate of spicy seafood deliciousness in front of me, and I got ready to make short work of it.

We stayed long enough that my three strong drinks wore off and I just felt weepy.

Darling and I had spent the last hour discussing our options to get into the rehab facility and see if the missing girls were somewhere inside. Darling called for a car to take her to her Marin County home.

Right before I closed her car door, she leaned over. "Gia, we don't got time. Those girls might end up dead like Layla if we don't get in that place."

I nodded. She was right.

"Let's talk in the morning," I said and kissed her cheek before closing the car door. "We'll go back tomorrow."

"What? You think they'll let us in this time?"

"I've got an idea."

I hoped it was too dark for her to spot the lie on my face.

WITHIN FIVE MINUTES OF GETTING HOME, I EMERGED FROM MY underground garage on my Kawasaki Ninja. The dark leather jacket and full-face helmet would not only provide me with some anonymity—something my black Ferrari could not do—but also it would allow me to easily escape if someone tried to tail me.

It took me ten minutes to make it back to Tompkins Avenue.

The neighborhood was quiet and dark.

The house seemed small from the street, but when I circled the block, I could tell from the side it was much larger. It had a backside that levered down the hill a few stories. I'd have to leave my bike on a street below and hike if I were going to be able to see the back of the house at all.

Maybe later. For now, I pulled up between two cars a few houses down and turned off my bike. Waiting. The rehab house had a front porch light. All the windows were black even though it was only nine at night. Then again, they might all have blackout curtains.

A low mist rolled in from the ocean, crawling up the street until it was between me and the house. A chill ran over me.

Whether it was from the cold or apprehension, I wasn't sure. I got off my bike, keeping my helmet on, and stretched. Then I made my way toward the house until I stood directly across from it. Too late, I noticed surveillance cameras tucked into the eaves. I ducked back into the shadows, but worried I'd already been made.

I was grateful for the helmet, thick motorcycle jacket, and boots that hid not only my identity but obscured my gender. At least I hoped they did.

The fog had made the night air ice cold, and I rubbed my leather clad arms trying to stay warm as I waited and watched from a recessed doorway. I was just about to give up and head home when the garage door slid open. I waited, holding my breath. The garage was a yawning dark space. My eyes strained to see into the darkness, hoping to see movement.

Who would make the first move? As the minutes stretched on, I decided it'd have to be me.

I took a step out of the doorway and onto the sidewalk and under the streetlight.

As I did, the headlights of a vehicle flashed on, illuminating me. I flinched slightly but tried to hide it. My throat was dry. Was it King? Would he show himself?

The engine gunned and the car came out of the dark garage so fast that I froze for a second before racing toward my motorcycle.

As the car zoomed past, I was already on the bike revving the engine. I caught up to it in time to see it round a corner down at the bottom of the hill. I wrenched the throttle, but then had to slam on the brakes around the next corner so I didn't lay the bike down. Damn streets of San Francisco. Soon, we were on flat land on Bryant Street, and I suddenly knew where the car was going. The Bay Bridge.

I had him.

Once he was on the bridge and I could ride the white line, I'd be able to not only keep up, but possibly even get a look inside the car.

For once, traffic was light getting onto the Bay Bridge. But as soon as we were up on the span, the lanes were clogged. That's when I remembered there had been a baseball game tonight. This must be the last of the crowd heading back to the East Bay.

I kept my eye on the black car as it merged into the fast lane a few cars ahead of me.

As soon as I cleared the onramp, I accelerated, and whipping my head side to side, made my move. Soon, I was threading the gap, riding the white line between the fast lane and the next lane over. I was nearly to the black car when a white sedan changed lanes right in front of me. I put on my brakes, narrowly avoiding a crash. My heart pounded in my throat. Adrenaline had heightened my senses, but it also made my hands tremble.

Once the white sedan was out of my way, I scanned the vehicles in front of me. The black car was now doing evasive maneuvers, zipping in and out of the fast lane to pass slower cars and once veering over to the slow lane to get around a small clump of pokey vehicles.

I needed to regain the momentum I'd lost from slowing. As if it were marked with a neon laser, my path through traffic appeared before me. It would take some concentration, but I could maneuver through it.

Right now, the driver of the red truck in front of me was either drunk or texting and didn't seem to be able to stay in the lines. It was my first obstacle. Once past it, I'd be able to accelerate. In front of the red truck, a massive blue SUV darted in and out of traffic. I didn't want it to decide to change lanes right when I was in its blind spot zipping by. I also needed to pass the SUV, before I felt comfortable gunning it. From there, I had a clear shot down the white line to the black car.

Accelerating to sixty miles per hour, I saw that the car next to the red truck had slowed down. I made my first move, zipping around the red truck. I took my foot off the gas to swerve around the SUV. Just as I passed, the SUV changed lanes, moving across the white line I had just been on.

Time to turn it on. I gunned the engine and hunkered down, head low, and gloved fingers gripping the handles of the bike. Glancing down at the speedometer, I knew I was pushing it. The speed limit on the bridge was fifty.

I'd only been riding for a few months. I'd taken classes at the Skip Barber Racing School but I wasn't an expert by any means. I silently prayed that the cars on either side of me would stay in their lanes until I caught up to the black car.

It was too much to ask for.

A beat-up, brown Chevy four cars ahead of me decided to change lanes. I was looking far enough ahead to react, but just barely. I managed to slide into the other lane, narrowly avoiding a crash.

The black car was now in front of me in the center lane. Seventy on a motorcycle on the Bay Bridge was pushing it. But then I crept up to eighty and I was finally beside the black car.

I pulled up alongside the driver's window and turned my helmeted head for a split second.

Dragon Lady was driving. She had a goddamn chauffeur's cap on her blonde head. Her hands tightly gripped the steering wheel. She shot me a snarky glance.

Even with my helmet on, she knew who I was.

Turning my attention back to the road, I saw we were coming up on a car in the left lane. It would be a narrow squeeze. As we grew closer, neck and neck, the other vehicle, a compact sports car, seemed to drift a little. I laid on my horn to keep it in its own lane. It jerked back to the left.

The black car easily passed it. The Dragon Lady glanced at

me and smiled at the same time she jerked the steering wheel, sending the car toward me. I managed to slow in time to get out of the way. The black car was now in front of me in the fast lane, up against the edge of the bridge. We were almost to the end of the span.

At first I began to creep up on the passenger side, but a large commercial truck hovered over my shoulder. It was so wide I was worried it would sideswipe me without trying. I came up on the narrow shoulder on the driver's side of the black car. This time I slowed near the back door. Seeing that the way in front of me was clear, I kept my grip steady on the handle bars and turned to look into the window. They were tinted, but I swore I could see a white shock of hair. My heart raced.

King.

Looking back in front of me, I saw that the narrow shoulder was disappearing. I could either accelerate in front of the black car or fall behind it. Before I could decide, Dragon Lady swerved again, cutting me off. This time I had nowhere to go.

Not wanting to lay my bike down, I gently squeezed the brakes, but as the black car brushed my thigh, I was forced to apply more pressure. I avoided the car, but immediately went into a skid. The bike wobbled and swerved. I kept a death grip on the handle and was managing to keep the bike upright when the black car decelerated until it was beside me again and this time forced me into the side of the bridge.

My handlebars smacked into the concrete and ricocheted me away.

I lost control, the bike skittering from side to side, as I struggled to stay upright while decelerating. But I couldn't do it. The black car disappeared into traffic just as the bike slipped out from under me. At that point, I'd slowed enough that the impact wasn't as bad as it might otherwise have been. I rolled and tucked hoping that I wouldn't end up in the lane beside me as road kill. I managed to roll and smashed into the wall. I sat up gingerly as people emerged from the cars that had stopped around me. I took off my helmet and examined the massive skid mark on it, stunned that I was still alive and furious that the black car was long gone.

8

I WAS CURSING AND FIGHTING AS THEY LOADED ME INTO THE ambulance.

"I'm fine."

I'd already answered all the questions about my name, the day, who the president was, and all those other questions checking for brain damage or concussion or whatever. I didn't want an ambulance ride. The EMT—a young guy with bright blue eyes and sandy brown hair, and who was easy on the eyes if not a little wet behind the ears—took my arm. "Listen. You need a ride anyway, right?"

I frowned. The last thing I wanted to remember was that my bike was totaled.

The second thing I didn't want to think about was that King had gotten away. Again.

"I can walk."

He laughed. "Then you'd be arrested and have a ride then, too. To jail."

"They wouldn't arrest me for walking on the Bay Bridge."

"They would," he said emphatically. He was so cute because he was so earnest.

"Wouldn't." I tried to hide my own grin.

"Let's just have the doc check you out. You might have hit your head harder than you think."

"No, I'm always like this," I said. But I let him put me in the back of the ambulance. "I don't want to lay down on that gurney."

He glanced at his colleague who shrugged. "Fine."

"We do need to check your vitals on the drive, though."

"Okay," I said as he shone a penlight into my eyes. Now that the adrenaline was dwindling, I was feeling really tired and less like resisting the ambulance ride.

"Do you want to call anyone?"

I dialed Darling.

"Oh, good Lord," she said. "Are you okay?"

"I'm fine. This nice young EMT wanted me to call and let someone know I'd been hurt. They're taking me to San Francisco United General, but I'll be fine. I'll call you when I finally get to go home."

"I'll come get you."

"No need. I'll take the bus or call a car."

"Gia..." Her motherly tone made me smile.

"Darling..." I said in the exact same tone. "I'll let you know when they are done poking and prodding me."

"Promise?"

"Yes," I said trying to sound annoyed.

After we hung up, I grimaced. My head didn't hurt, but my leg did. I looked down and saw the leg of my pants shredded, and a bandage peeked out from behind the tattered material. I hadn't really been paying attention when the EMT had patched me up.

The cute one noticed my gaze. "That's going to need stitches."

"Great." I was pissed. Stitches in my thigh would impede my Budo training.

When we pulled up to emergency, my scowl grew bigger.

James stood in the middle of the roundabout with his arms crossed. He was wearing his police uniform and looked imposing.

He must've had the early shift this morning. Was it already morning? Sure enough the sky was lightening as I thought it.

When they opened the ambulance doors, I felt a pang of guilt when I saw the concerned look in his eyes. He tried to hide it and said in a gruff voice. "You okay?"

I nodded.

The EMTs exchanged glances.

I tried to stand, but the one EMT held up his hand. I didn't argue as they put me in a wheelchair and wheeled me in the doors

It wasn't until they left us alone in an exam room that I exhaled loudly. "I'm sorry. It's a long story."

He raised an eyebrow. "Looks like we've got time."

I spilled it all right before a doctor examined my leg and asked me the same questions the EMT had.

"We could do an MRI to check your head. A brain bleed can sometimes sneak up on us." He was older with gray at the temples and a tiny little moustache. He looked competent.

"I'm good."

"Let's just stitch up this leg then and get you home."

When he was finished putting a measly five stitches in, he said the nurse would be in shortly with my discharge papers.

As soon as he walked out, James stood and paced. "You're pretty sure it's King?"

"Yes."

He headed for the curtain, pulling it aside.

"Where you going?" I said, scrambling to get off the exam table.

"Welfare check at that address you gave me."

I grinned. "I'm coming too."

Wincing as I put pressure on my leg, I snatched my leather jacket and phone off the chair.

"You can't come. You're not discharged yet."

I rolled my eyes and headed toward the exit.

———

WE PEERED into the windows to the front of the building. The curtains were gone. The view inside revealed a completely empty space.

"What the hell?" I said. "There were thick curtains on all the windows just hours ago."

"Looks like your questions sent them running," he said. "Not to mention following King last night."

"Fuck. Fuck. Fuck." I wanted to punch something. Now King was in the wind—again— and the girls were gone.

A neighbor came out to his car and glanced over at the squad car.

James walked toward him. I stayed behind. I figured it was professional courtesy. Let him do his job without his nosy girlfriend asking questions. But I was dying to find out what the man was saying.

Finally, James came back over. He didn't speak until the man pulled away.

"A moving truck showed up in the middle of the night. Sounds like not long after you started tailing the car. More than a dozen men loaded the truck up and drove away. Whole thing took less than an hour."

"Did he see any people? Any young women?"

"No, but he said that a big old SUV pulled into the garage when the moving truck arrived and left a few minutes later. The windows were tinted, and he couldn't see inside."

I thought of something. I went to the front door and tried the handle. It turned.

"Hey!" James said as I walked inside.

I was already peering in a series of rooms that lined a hall when he caught up.

"You can't be in here."

"Why? It's not breaking and entering if the door's unlocked."

"It's trespassing."

"Is it?" I raised an eyebrow. It probably was, but I didn't care.

I was disappointed to find that every single room was empty. There was some debris on the floor, little scraps of paper and dust. I crouched down, wincing as my leg with the stitches bent, and poked at a scrap of paper. It was a candy wrapper. For a Big Chunk candy bar. Made by Arabelle Sweets Company in Oakland.

James's radio crackled. He leaned down to the mic on his shoulder and said something. All I could make out was the name of the street we were on and "welfare check."

My phone rang. I glanced down. Darling.

I clicked answer and spoke before she could. "You like calling my boyfriend behind my back and telling him my business? Because I got a whole hell of a lot of info I could give George?" I was half joking.

"Now you just simmer down," she said. "He has a right to know when his girl gets in a car accident and is going to the hospital."

"I didn't say he didn't. It's just my job to be a good girlfriend and keep him from worrying."

"Oh, Gia. If being a good girlfriend was your job, you'd have been fired a long time ago."

I scowled. "What do you want anyway?"

She cackled with laughter, pleased as punch that she'd gotten a rise out of me.

"I had one of my associates find out who owns that house."

"You're good, Darling. Nosy as fuck, but good. I'll give you that."

That laugh again.

"It's owned by some holding company, Cagney & Lacey or something."

"Oh really," I said and it was my turn to laugh. "I doubt that's the name."

"Well something close to that."

"Can we trace it or connect it to King?"

"That's what we're working on sugar pie. But you stay away from there until I find out more, you hear?"

"Too late."

"Gia!" She shrieked it, then said something that shook me to the core. "It's time we call the police and have them come take a look around. Maybe get the girls out for us."

I'd never once in all the years I'd known Darling heard her suggest calling the police. I was stunned.

"We need to get those girls out of that house now," she said. "We need to call the cops and get them to go to that house. Otherwise more are going to end up like Layla."

I slumped against the wall. An image of that mother's haunted eyes and the tiny body in the hospital bed brought tears to my eyes. "I'm here now."

"Gia, you stay away from that house. Wait for the police."

"I'm here with James. But get this—it's empty. A moving van showed up shortly after the black car left and cleared the place out."

"Oh no." I could hear the defeat in her voice.

"Yeah. Sorry. It looks like if there were any girls here they left in an SUV about the same time that the van showed up."

Darling exhaled. "I was hoping maybe the police would raid it and they'd find those girls. I really don't want to tell their mommas we got nothing."

I thought again of that tiny body hooked up to all the machines, clinging to life. And here Darling was already preparing to tell them it was too late.

"It's not over yet."

9

I CURLED UP NEXT TO JAMES AND WE STAYED IN BED ALL DAY, BUT only after convincing him that the doctor didn't have any concerns with me sleeping after the concussion. Still, he woke me up twice to check my pupils.

We both needed the sleep. He'd worked the night shift, and I'd been busy going after King so neither one of us had slept the night before. When we awoke and decided to get up, the sun was setting.

James made me scrambled eggs with chorizo for dinner, insisting I sit up in bed while he worked.

"This is all very sweet, but I'm fine," I said, watching James work.

Django nuzzled his muzzle into my thigh and gave a loud sigh.

I couldn't believe he wasn't over at my galley kitchen begging for scraps. The chorizo smelled like heaven.

"Let me help," I started to get up.

"No way," he said, swatting at me with a dish towel. "Besides, it won't kill you to relax for once."

"How do you know?"

He rolled his eyes.

"I've been relaxing," I said.

It was a lie. I worked nonstop. My passion project, Ethel's Place—mixed-use housing for the homeless—had taken off. We were developing projects all across the country. The concept wasn't terribly unique, but it seemed to fill a niche. We built apartment buildings with residences upstairs and small retailers on the ground level. The residents worked in the businesses on the street level and then received training to eventually move out and support themselves.

I'd been so busy growing the business, it was difficult to find time for anything else. James was good for me. Ever since I started seeing him again a few months ago, he made me slow down. He made me keep my dates with him and relax.

But sometimes it was hard.

"I'm having a hard time relaxing thinking about Layla."

He looked down at the stove where he was poking some eggs around.

"Yeah," he said.

"I wish we had a lead."

The neighbor had given James the name of the moving company, but when James tried to track it down he found more than 100 trucks had been rented in the Bay Area in the past two days. It would be next to impossible to trace which truck the neighbor had seen.

Darling's contact had investigated the name on the lease for the house, but that had also led to a dead end because it was registered to some Caribbean business offshore that was most likely a shell company.

But all these dead ends told me one thing: The more obscure and odd it got, the more I was convinced it was King up to his tricks.

I was frustrated but obediently ate my dinner.

When we were finished, James washed the dishes and checked his watch.

"I've got to go to work. You sure you're going to be okay?"

I nodded from my bed. I wore big, cozy flannel pajamas, and he'd propped up all the pillows on my side and had a carafe of water and a teapot on my nightstand.

"Yes," I said, feigning a yawn.

"I really don't like the idea of leaving you alone after the accident."

"Even the doctor said I probably didn't hit my head hard enough to do any serious damage.

"'Probably' being the operative word." A crease appeared between his brows. "And I don't recall him saying that."

He was such a mother hen. It was something I adored about him even though it was slightly annoying for someone like me who's basically alone in the world. I hated it and loved it simultaneously. His mother must've raised him right. Thinking of his mother sent a flush of guilt over me.

"James?"

He paused in the doorway. "I'm sure I blew it with your mom skipping out without saying goodbye, huh?"

"It didn't exactly make the best impression."

I winced.

"I told her your friend had an emergency. I think she at least respects that."

"What?"

"That you're a good and loyal friend." He came and sat down on the edge of my bed. He'd taken off his uniform shirt to fix me dinner, and the wife beater he had on underneath left nothing to the imagination. I leaned into his chest inhaling deeply.

"You got some powerful pheromones." I began kissing his side.

He groaned in response. Soon he was all mine in my bed. An

hour later, he'd taken a shower and was sitting on the edge of the bed rubbing my back.

"That feels so good, baby," I said.

He stood. "I got to go. Call me if you start to get even a little headache. Promise."

I nodded, meeting his eyes in the mirror.

"Promise."

As soon as I heard the front door close, I threw back the covers. I'd keep my promise to call him if my head hurt. But I'd never promised to stay home in bed.

While James was in the shower earlier getting ready for work, I'd replayed our visit to the house.

I'd closed my eyes and envisioned the walk through the house and then paused in the bedroom. Something had stuck out in that room. Something that was gnawing at my memory. Something wasn't quite right, and for the life of me I couldn't figure out what it was. I mean, the room was empty. There wasn't even a whole lot to take in. But something told me to go back and look harder and deeper.

James had been sketchy about me going in the house the first time so I didn't want to go back with him or tell him my plan. But somehow, I'd known I might want to go back because I'd watched James twist the lock on the door as he waited for me to come out. But I'd bent down and fiddled with a shoelace for so long, he gave up and stepped out first—long enough for me to unlock the door and then slam it behind us. Then, I'd grabbed his hand and walked toward the car to make sure he didn't double check that the door was locked.

With my bike smashed to shit, I needed to drive my fun car. I parked my Ferrari a few houses down from the rehab house on Tompkins, cursing the fact that even though I had the most low-profile Ferrari on the streets with its matte black paintjob, it was still a goddamn quarter-million-dollar sports car and sure to attract the attention of nosy neighbors. But I hadn't wanted to wait around for a car service. I was itching to get back into the house.

Under the cover of darkness, I crept along the opposite sidewalk watching all the neighbor's windows, but the lights remained out and the curtains closed. So far so good.

Crossing the street, I still didn't hear a sound. It was a quiet neighborhood. The doorknob to the front door turned easily in my palm. I slipped inside and shut the door quickly behind me, locking it. I shuffled several paces to the side and crouched, leaning against the wall and holding my breath. If someone attacked or fired at the door, I'd be off to one side and low in the shadows.

The cold, hard metal of the gun pressed to the small of my back felt reassuring. For a second, I considered taking it out and holding it before me, but then I'd be gripping both a gun and a flashlight. Right now, I had no reason to be holding the gun, so I kept my arms in a defensive pose, ready for an attack until my eyes adjusted to the dim interior.

I wouldn't put it past King to be lurking here inside somewhere, waiting to trap me and kill me. After waiting at least two full minutes, my eyes had adjusted to the dark and I could make out the interior of the room from the streetlights filtering through the large front window. The room was empty.

Now that I could see better and was ready to move, I took out my gun and held it before me. I stuck the flashlight in my waistband so I could grip my pistol with two hands.

Instead of heading straight toward the hallway leading to the bedrooms, I made a wide circuit, keeping to the walls opposite with my eyes trained on that darker entryway. Every nerve in my body was electric, alert to any sign of danger.

Again, I thought that King knew me well enough to know I

might return here and it would be perfectly evil of him to be waiting in the dark for me.

I flicked on the flashlight. The hall was empty. I held the flashlight in the left hand, gun in the right, stabilized on my left forearm so I could aim the light forward. I checked in each room and closet. Empty. It wasn't until I'd cleared the entire house that I relaxed.

Now I could actually investigate the bedroom toward the back that had caught my attention. It was where I'd found the candy wrapper. But there was more to my intuition than just a piece of garbage on the floor.

I walked into the room, glanced around, and then closed my eyes, thinking about the impression burned on my eyelid—my inner eye roving over what I'd just seen. It was a room with wood paneling from floor to ceiling. Dingy grayish carpet. A closet with a single open door so I could see inside it as soon as I entered the room. One small window facing the canyon behind the house. Tiny bars even though the window was up high and too small for the average teenager to squeeze through.

I opened my eyes again. There was *something* here. But what? My mind was seeing something that my eyes weren't registering. I remembered a forensic science class I'd taken once with the county medical examiner. He showed us a piece of drywall taken from a home where an infant had reportedly rolled off a bed, fractured his skull, and died. The drywall looked like a normal piece of drywall until he held up a special light to it. There was a perfectly round indentation on the piece of drywall, nearly invisible to the naked eye, that was the exact size and shape of the infant's head.

I'd use touch. I took my hands and placed my palms flat waist high and ran them around the room. There were scuff marks where it looked like headboards and other furniture had knocked against the wooden paneling. It was near one of these scuff marks that I felt a bump in the paneling. I tried to pry it up, but it wouldn't budge. I leaned down and found if I scooted the carpet back a bit I could pry the panel of wood back a little. As I did, a wad of folded notebook paper fell to the floor beside me.

My heart raced.

I carefully unfolded the yellow notebook paper and began to read the first sheet. It was a letter addressed to a Jamal. I flipped to the last page. It was from a girl named Serafina.

The first page was dated two months ago, the last page yesterday.

"Might as well write you as I ain't ever gone get out of here. He told me that moving in here meant all the Monkey I want. And it's true. I get dosed every day. Like it's a vitamin. But something's going on here. There's girls disappearing. Like this one girl who was here when I first got here. One morning at breakfast she just didn't show up. I was asking that pale fucker with the red eyes questions when he came to visit and Blondie told me later to shut up. She flashed her big fancy Louis Vuitton and showed me them big diamonds on her fingers and said when you join up with Mr. King, you get all those things if you show you're loyal. All I said, was "What? You got a few fancy things, but you a receptionist at a jail for girls on drugs? I could do better.""

I froze reading this passage. It was right there in black and white. King. I raced through the next part:

"She didn't like me talking back. I thought she was going to kill me right then, but she only sighed and left. It was that one big dude—the guy with the shaved head—who tried to kill me. He slapped me so hard my head hit the wall, and I think I might have blacked out. And then he grabbed my boobs while I was on the floor, twisting them so hard I cried. He was going for my privates when the pale dude walked in and he jumped back from me like I was on fire. The weird white dude walked right up to that big guy and slapped him across the face. I never seen that guy again. Thank God. But Blondie, she told me the next day that I'd be sorry for that. That the big guy was her favorite and I'd regret it now that he was gone."

I skimmed to the last page. I didn't find anything else revealing until the end. Mainly complaints about the food and reports of arguments with the other girls over what to watch on TV. Then, I read the page dated yesterday.

"Blondie told us that we might have to have sex with some of the men who are working there. To keep them happy. And that we can't tell King. That's nothing new for me. But Josie though, she was all wide-eyed and worried. I heard her crying in her bed at night. I almost felt bad for her. But as my Nonna says, don't drive the truck if you can't shift the gears. What she thinks that she can be miss innocent and still do the Oxy? I don't feel sorry for her. You want to get high, you pay the price. And now she hooked like the rest of us. She's lucky she got away because of Layla.

The first mention of Layla made my heart pound.

"That girl was drooling when they carried her out of here. She dead. There's no way she's coming back. I saw it. They gave her too much. I heard her screaming in that one locked room at the end of the hall, but they did it anyway. They wanted her to O.D.

"And now Josie disappeared. Blondie was so mad. Then the pale fucker hit her. Slapped her right in the TV room. Right across the face. And you know what that crazy bitch did? She laughed. She laughed and fell down laughing."

I tucked the note into my back pocket and shivered, looking around. It was almost as if the man's presence lingered in the rooms where he had been.

The note proved King was involved and contained a lot of good information. But I wondered if it could help me figure out who the other girls were who'd been held here—and I was lucky —where they were taken. I'd re-read it and examine it again at home.

I felt sorry for the girl despite her seemingly hard shell. It was a little girl putting on bravado, trying to justify her circumstances and the choices that had led her there. But the reality was, doing drugs was a fucked-up choice, but it didn't mean that the girls had given consent to be raped and used as sex slaves. Not by a long shot.

And it didn't mean that they wanted to die.

I heard a bang and car doors slamming. I scrambled to my feet, flicked off the light, and raced to the hall. I peeked around the corner and could see through the big window to the street. Cops. Two squads. Lit up.

Neighbors must have called.

I was certain one of the cops was planning on circling around the back of the house. It was common procedure so burglars wouldn't bail out the back door. I had no time to waste. Whirling, I took in the main room. There was a door near the kitchen. A side door. It might work.

But it would mean crossing the empty main room. And the flashlights were already bobbing, heading my way. I ducked and ran toward the door. The doorknob turned easily under my fingers, and I slipped through just as I heard the front door creak open. Glancing around, I decided to head into the neighbor's yard instead of down the hillside. Any burglar would try to get as far away from the cops as possible. That wasn't my aim.

I wanted to spy on them. I ducked through the neighbor's yard and then hopped a small fence through another neighbor's pool area, hoping they didn't have dogs before I came back up through a side yard onto the street near my Ferrari.

Instead of hopping in my car, I casually strolled over to it, keeping an eye on the flashlights inside the house. Soon the lights turned on and I heard a cop shout, "Clear."

I leaned against my car and lit a cigarette, waiting and watching.

After a few minutes, an officer came huffing and puffing around the corner of the house and entered through the front door. I clocked four cops.

Only then did I slip into my car, closing the door softly behind me and slumping in my seat. When the officers came out, I ducked all the way down until I heard the two squad cars pull away.

I waited to the count of 100 and then started my engine. It took a five-point turn to get oriented the right way on the narrow street. It was only as I was pulling away that I noticed a face in a car parked facing the opposite direction. My heart lurched, and I slammed on my breaks. But it was too late, the vehicle—a small black car with dark, tinted windows—had pulled smoothly out of its parking spot and was disappearing in the opposite direction. I threw my car in reverse and began following it, eyes on my rearview mirror until we came to a sharp curve and I had to slam on my brakes to prevent slamming into the tightly parked cars. My driving skills were more advanced than the average person, but only when I was driving forward. In reverse, I was about as good as any other bozo, which meant not at all. As I swore and watched the other car's tail lights disappear, I made a vow to change that.

I slammed my fist into the steering wheel. Once again, King had gotten away. Because even though I'd only gotten the tiniest glimpse of the man when my headlights flashed on, it was enough to see a shock of white hair. The Albino had been watching me and waiting.

What the fuck was his game?

10

I slipped back into my loft and my bed before dawn.

When James arrived, exhausted from working all night, I held out my arms to welcome him to my warm bed.

We both slept until noon.

I woke first. While the coffee was percolating, Django and I ran out to get almond croissants. James was still snoring.

He was still motionless when I returned. I was sitting at my café table watching him sleep, nibbling a croissant, and sucking down my coffee when my phone rang, startling me. James stirred and mumbled, but didn't wake.

It was Darling. I snatched up the phone and whispered urgently, "What you got?"

"One of Layla's friend's came to the back room of my salon today with her momma and had some things to say. Her name is Wanda." She paused dramatically and took a deep breath.

"Keep talking."

"Good Lord, woman. You are the most impatient person I've ever met."

"Yada yada. I know, I know. Just tell me what Wanda had to say."

"She says Layla got ahold of a phone one night last week and texted her. Told her she was prisoner in some house. It wasn't a rehab. They were dosing them with drugs every day."

Darling sounded outraged.

Even though this was just further confirmation of what I'd read in Serafina's letter, I said, "Fuckers."

"Lordie, you have a foul mouth, Gia."

"So, sue me."

"Anyway, Layla didn't want the drugs anymore. Wanda says she just wanted to go home, but then they started restraining her and forcing them on her. She wanted to get out. She texted Wanda to get help. But Wanda thinks she got caught. I guess Layla was using some woman's phone while the woman was smoking outside. And they punished her by giving her an overdose."

Everything Darling said matched up with what I'd read in the note left by the other girl.

"Layla asked Wanda not to tell her mom but to come get her. She was going to try to break out."

James stirred again, this time sitting up, yawning, and stretching. He looked over at me, and I said pointedly to Darling, "King is running a rehab house for girls hooked on opioids except instead of getting them off the drugs, he keeps them dosed. I just can't figure out why."

James nodded and scratched his bare chest. He didn't seem surprised at what I'd just said.

Everything had pointed in this direction.

"What we need to find out is where he moved the teens."

"Their mommas are worried sick," Darling said.

"I can only imagine." I thought for a second and remembered the note I found. "Is one of them named Serafina?"

"No," Darling said. "The girls I know about are Nichelle and Dania."

Based on the number of bedrooms—three—and marks on the walls from the headboards, I'd guessed that each room held two girls. That meant at least six girls could be held there at a time

A small enough number to fit in that SUV that SUV the neighbor saw leaving the scene the same night the movers had come.

James was up now.

"Listen, Darling. I gotta go. Keep me posted."

James was reaching for his clothes when I stopped him with a kiss.

Soon we were both back in bed. I could never get enough of him.

I'd read something about how we are attracted to people with opposite immune systems so, that when those two people have a child, they combine a powerful set of immune systems to keep propagating the species. If that was true, maybe it explained the powerful attraction between me and James. I couldn't stay away from him. No matter how hard I tried.

But it was deeper than that. I cared for him so much, but I wasn't ready to commit.

Later, lying in bed beside him as the shadows grew long, I stared at the ceiling. I knew why I couldn't commit to James. It had nothing to do with anything lacking in him and everything to do with me worrying about hurting him. But even more than that, it had to do with Bobby.

Bobby was dead because of me. He had been the love of my life. He'd been the first person I'd ever imagined having a family with. Even though James was the most nurturing man I'd ever met, I couldn't for the life of me imagine having a child with him. It wasn't something I wanted anymore. Not then. Maybe not ever.

But Bobby? I'd imagined growing old with him.

And now he was dead. Forever young because of me.

Everyone I loved died. And usually a horrible, violent death —murdered.

I was still astonished that my best friend, Dante, was alive and well. But Dante lived up north, and we didn't get to see each other often. Maybe that physical distance was somehow keeping him safe from the chaos in my life. And maybe by keeping my distance from James, I was saving him too.

By keeping my distance from James maybe I was saving his life.

Sometimes, though, like right now, I was weak. I wanted to give myself fully to him. Even if it was only for now. The one thing holding me back was Bobby.

Until I found a way to make peace with his death, I would never let down my guard.

I'd talked to Darling about it one day.

She told me that I should build an altar, an *ofrenda*, this year for the Day of the Dead. I would make it and then bring it to Garfield Park on the actual *Dia de los Muertos*. There was a procession that ended at the park. Once there, I could invite Bobby's spirit back to me and ask his forgiveness. She told me I needed to do that if I were ever going to be able to move on.

I told her to keep her creepy, voodoo, Day of the Dead shit to herself, but part of me wondered...November second was only a few weeks away.

James stood up suddenly. "I've got to go home. Feed Snuffles."

"Aw, you should've just brought him over. Django and I miss him."

Snuffles had belonged to a man who tried to kill me— Damien Thornwell. A legend in the Silicon Valley tech world who had died by my hand before realizing his dream of living in space.

After I'd thrown him into the rotors of a helicopter on a hotel rooftop in Rio, I'd felt sorry for his dog and took him in. But when I started seeing James again, I realized the damn dog loved him more, so I gave him up. It was the best thing ever to watch James as a dog-daddy. His mother had kept an immaculate house and never wanted a dog when he was growing up because she thought they were "dirty." Another reason I'd doubted we could ever get along.

Now Snuffles was his baby.

"Well, you better get home. Poor thing probably cried for you all day."

He looked ashamed. "I hate to say it but maybe I shouldn't own a dog."

"I was teasing," I said and sat up. "You pay that college kid to come in and walk him and love on him during the day. It's fine."

"I still feel bad leaving him alone so much. Plus, I've got to take my blood pressure meds."

"I thought you had a spare bottle here?" I started to head to the bathroom to hunt in the medicine cabinet.

"I need to refill that one."

"Go on, then," I said with a disappointed sigh. I helped him find his clothes and then pushed him toward the door. "We'll catch up later."

He kissed me on the forehead and was gone.

As soon as the door slammed, I grabbed my jeans and took out the note and candy wrapper. I hadn't told James about either of them. I'd gotten into the bad habit of keeping things from him.

It wasn't that I was trying to deceive him, but sometimes James was too goody-goody. He didn't approve of anything that bordered on illegal, and sometimes those borderline activities served me well.

He was a cop. I was someone who'd sometimes operated outside the law.

And to make it crystal clear, I was a murderer. I'd killed and gotten away with it.

Of course, in my eyes, every time had been justified. Every. Time.

But still.

James had taken an oath.

I didn't hesitate to break the law if I thought it would best serve justice.

Like in this instance. When I thought of what King was doing to those teenage girls, I knew I would do anything to find them and stop him from doing it to anyone else. I would use any means necessary to prevent another death like Layla's.

I didn't know how we were going to find the girls, but something told me that King wanted me to do so. Or, at least to find him. But why?

I mean, sure, I'd basically ruined his life and drove him into hiding forever, but what was all this about? If he wanted me dead, why not just try to kill me?

But something deep down told me that it was more than that to him. He wanted to toy with me. I was a pawn in his game, and he was enjoying manipulating me.

That's why he'd left the candy wrapper for me to find.

King was much too meticulous to clean out an entire house in an hour and yet leave one candy wrapper. At first, I'd assumed that one of the movers had been snacking and tossed it aside. But the more I thought about it, the more I was certain that King would've done a walkthrough of the place to make sure no evidence was left behind. If he hadn't done it himself, he would've had someone competent and trustworthy do it for him. There was no way he would leave something like that behind unless he wanted me to find it.

11

KING WAS EXCEEDINGLY SMART AND EXCRUCIATINGLY CAREFUL. HE left nothing to chance. After all, he'd had a moving truck and entire crew either on standby or had the power to rally people as soon as he saw me stalking the house. But that wrapper had been left behind.

For a reason.

For me to find.

It was a clue. Or, rather, it was a bread crumb left for me to find.

I examined it.

It was made by Arabelle Sweets Company. In Oakland. In the East Bay. Across the Bay Bridge. The last direction I'd seen King going.

I grabbed my car keys. Fine.

I'd bite.

THE SUN WAS SETTING behind me, its reddish golden glow sparkling on the waves of the bay as I drove across the Bay Bridge.

I zipped my Ferrari around slower cars but wasn't in a big hurry. Few people headed to the East Bay on a Saturday night, so traffic was light. Instead, the span of the bridge coming *into* the city from the suburbs was stop-and-go traffic. The line of cars waiting to get on the Bay Bridge probably backed up into the Oakland Hills.

Of course traffic was much lighter than the other night when I wrecked my bike. I still had a tender spot on my head, and the stitches in my thigh throbbed a little, but for the most part I'd forgotten about the crash entirely.

My speakers blared Camilla Cabello.

Her lyrics spoke to me. Especially the ones about wanting a true friend in a sea of vipers. Tell me about it, *chica*.

I adored my friends, but really craved a female best friend. Darling was more like a mother figure to me. I wanted someone my age to hang with. To complain about James to. Stuff like that.

I'd met someone who I knew could easily fit the bill, but Sydney Rye lived on some tropical island somewhere. She was the first woman I'd met who I felt like I knew instantly. She'd killed. She fought for justice no matter what the cost. She had honed her body to a well-oiled fighting machine. In other words, we were the same.

My phone rang, interrupting Cabello's throaty voice.

Dante. My friend since high school. I had no problem making dude friends. Or keeping them.

"Yo," I said.

"Hey, *amici*? What are you up to?"

"Driving." I glanced at the clock on my dashboard. "How can you possibly be calling me on a Saturday night?"

Dante owned two uber-successful restaurants in Calistoga, and Saturday night was crunch time.

"I'm in Cuba."

"You're kidding?"

"Not. I'm doing research for my next restaurant. And recruiting some chefs. Next place is going to be Cuban food."

"Oh my God. I love you. Can I move in and sleep above the restaurant? By the way, I'm listening to Camilla Cabello right now"

Silence.

"She's Cuban!"

"Oh." He chuckled politely. He'd obviously never heard of her, which was insane. "Speaking of sleeping above the restaurant—that's why I was calling. Can you think of anyone from Ethel's Place who might help me staff the place? You don't need to give me an answer immediately. Just start thinking. I've got Silas on it, too."

Silas was his sweet, former boy toy who now was one of Dante's best platonic friends and managed one of his restaurants.

"That sounds amazing," I said.

"What else is new? You still seeing James?"

"Yes." My voice had grown quiet.

"Gia?"

"Long story. But the big news is that King is back."

It was his turn to grow silent.

Neither of us spoke for a second and then he said, "I can have a ticket waiting for you at the airport. I think I need your help picking the right chef. You have great instincts about people and I need that savviness right now. I mean, I'm going to spend a lot of money relocating a chef and his entire family."

"It's okay," I said. "I can handle King."

"Gia."

"Dante, you know you don't really need my help. You just want to whisk me off to safety."

"I do need your help. I swear."

"Dante." My voice was firm.

"But yeah, I'll admit, I want you the hell out of there."

"How's this," I said, "once I wrap up this situation, I'll take you up on that offer and come help you down in Cuba. How long you going to be there?"

"Another ten days."

"Perfect. See you soon."

I hung up before he could argue.

12

THE ADDRESS FOR THE CANDY COMPANY WAS IN AN AREA OF Oakland I'd only seen on the news. It was near where an entire warehouse had recently burned to the ground killing thirty-six ravers.

My eyes narrowed as I passed the charred remains that had become a semi-permanent memorial site. Dubbed the Ghost Ship, a green fence surrounded the building and was laden with flowers, notes, T-shirts, posters, and pictures.

A few blocks over was the giant warehouse with the small "Arabelle Sweets Company" sign out front. I circled the block, looking into the other parked cars, trying to sniff out a trap.

King wanted me there, so it made sense that he or one of his henchmen would be lying in wait. But nothing seemed out of the ordinary.

It was a misfit neighborhood. Old row houses next to small industrial buildings. As I cruised past, I caught the attention of a group of guys loitering on the porch of one house.

Circling the block, I parked behind the building and walked around looking for a way in. There was only a garage door and one main entry in the front. It didn't seem suspicious. It didn't' seem anything. But King had drawn me here for a reason. I just needed to figure out what it was.

The group at the house stayed in the shadows, but I knew they were curious about what I was up to. I got back in the Ferrari and came back around to the front, pulling into a spot directly across the street.

I got out and leaned on my car. Waiting.

There was some loud heckling and laughing, but I didn't move.

Finally, one of them got the nerve to come over to me.

I lifted my chin in acknowledgment. I reached into my leather jacket and the boy startled.

Because he was a boy. Maybe late teens but not quite a man yet.

His friends trailed behind in the shadows.

He was reaching for something in his back waistband when he saw what I'd grabbed. A baggie with a blunt and a pack of matches.

Without taking my eyes off him, I extracted the blunt and put it between my lips.

He stood about five feet in front of me, cocking his head.

"Hey," I said and struck a match to light my blunt.

Snickers came from the group behind him.

"You sure you want to park right here?"

I nodded.

"This place isn't safe for girls like you," he wove closer. Not walking in a straight line. "Especially girls who drive cars like that"

Behind him, I saw figures splitting off to each side. I didn't let on that I'd seen them.

"You should probably get the fuck out of here?" He phrased it like a question. He was scared.

I took a big drag on the blunt and exhaled slowly before answering. "Why?"

He sputtered. He didn't have an answer. Someone behind him said, "We'll fuck you up. Take your weed and your mother-fucking Maserati."

"It's a Ferrari douchebag," someone else said.

I smiled now. A big grin that took the boy in front of me off guard. He took a step back.

"You think that's funny?"

I nodded.

He scowled.

"Why don't you boys just settle down and help me smoke this weed I brought as a peace offering." I held the baggie up and shook it. It contained several other joints. Even in the dim light from the streetlight, they could tell it wasn't nothing to sneeze at.

One boy in the back whistled appreciatively.

"Peace offering, huh?" the boy in front of me said. He wore an Irish fisherman's cap and a slouchy sweatshirt.

"Sure. We can call it that."

Someone behind him said something, and he nodded.

"Fine," he said. "Throw it over here."

"Come get it."

"No fucking way."

"Okay. Fair enough." I reached out with my hand with the bag toward him. He snatched the bag and backed up a few paces before opening it and smelling it. Then his eyes narrowed.

"You a cop?"

I scoffed. "Um, do you read the newspaper? It's legal now."

"Whatever."

I shrugged. "To answer your question, no, I'm not a cop. I just got some questions about that warehouse over there." I jutted my chin toward the Arabelle Sweets Company.

"Like what?" He passed the bag back to somebody behind him.

"You see anything odd there lately."

"I don't live here."

"Who does?"

"Ricky."

"Where's Ricky?"

He gestured behind him, but then said, "He ain't gonna talk to you right here in front of everyone?"

"Why not?"

"It's the way it is."

"Ask Ricky if he wants to go for a ride?" I leaned over and opened my driver's side door.

"What the fuck?" someone said.

The boy in front of me made a face. "How we know you not some fucking pervert take him and never come back?"

I thought about it for a minute. "I guess you don't."

We sat there for a minute, and I heard whispering behind him.

"I tell you what," I said. "You seem like a smart kid…"

He scowled at the word "kid" but seemed to stand a little straighter.

"I bet you have some really good gut instincts about people. What's your gut tell you about me?"

He burst into laughter. "You're a crazy motherfucker."

I nodded. "Maybe. But do you think I would hurt your friend?"

He cocked his head and then slowly shook it. "Nah."

"Okay, then."

He stepped back into the dark recesses and a minute later, a younger boy, maybe fourteen emerged from the group. I got into the driver's seat and started fiddling with the radio.

"What kind of music you like, Ricky?"

"I like everything." He sounded bashful.

"Got it," I said. I popped in a Metallica CD. "Get in and let's see how well this baby does on Oakland streets."

He looked behind him for a second but then the uncertainty disappeared and he hopped in my passenger seat. I watched him scramble to find the seat belt, and my heart melted a little.

Right before we pulled out the other guy came and leaned in the window.

"I wrote down your license plate number."

I smiled. "Like I said, you aren't no dummy. We'll be back soon."

Then I peeled out, leaving a little bit of my tire tread and some smoke behind us. I glanced over at the kid beside me and saw a big grin spread across his face.

"Don't worry, Ricky. I'm trained in race car driving. We're gonna have some fun."

Forty-five minutes later, we were back onto the street. The group of guys jumped off the porch and ran over, excited. All their bravado gone. I hopped out and met the older boy face to face.

"What's your name?" he asked.

"Gia."

I leaned forward and shook his hand.

"Johnny."

"Thanks for making that happen, Johnny," I said and turned toward the car door.

"Like I had a choice," he mumbled, then said louder, "Can I ask you something?"

I paused.

"You smiled when I said we were gonna fuck you up."

I waited.

"Why?"

Pushing aside my leather jacket, I could see his eyes widen as he took in the Sig Sauer P238 tucked in its holster. I was not fucking around.

He laughed and swore.

I crooked a finger. He leaned in. "I told Ricky to call me if he sees anything fucked up at that building, but just so you know, you see a dude with all-white hair around here, stay out of his way. He's pure evil."

He nodded seriously.

I squealed away without waiting for an answer.

Ricky had told me during our outing that every morning at seven, a chubby dude arrived at the building and unlocked the front door. He knew because it happened every day as he walked to the bus stop to catch the number eleven bus so he'd make it to school on time.

He attended some charter school for genius, prodigy kids. He seemed ashamed when he talked about it, but the more we chatted, he said he felt like an oddball there because all the other students were rich.

What Ricky had relayed gave me a plan. James was working a double—filling in for a buddy who'd called in sick.

I'd go home and catch a few hours' sleep and then be back at the warehouse at six, finding a good spot to seem inconspicuous. And that meant no Ferrari. Ricky told me his mom would've already left for work by then, so I could park it in their garage if I got there right at six. But I had a better idea. Ricky was 16 and had a driver's license. So, I was going to let Ricky drive my car to school. See what those snotty little kids thought of that.

And from what I knew of him in the short time we'd spent together, I knew he'd treat my car with kid's gloves. And if he didn't? Wouldn't be the end of the world. I was getting a little tired of having such a high-profile ride. It seemed like nowadays everything I did required me to be more incognito.

The next morning, I pulled into his driveway. He came out with sleep in his eyes and wet hair. He had on a school uniform—beige pants and a light blue polo—and my heart softened a bit more.

I tossed him the keys.

"Why don't you take her to school today? I'll meet you back here at three?"

The car keys had landed smack in his open palms, but he dropped them in astonishment.

"What?"

"You heard me. Call me if you have any problems. I'll be close by."

I took off walking toward the warehouse, ignoring the astonished noises he was making behind me.

Last night, I'd scoped out the building directly across from the candy company. It was abandoned. This morning, armed with a crowbar, I headed to the alley. It was easy to pry the board off the door and slip inside. I took out a flashlight and made my way through the dust and cobwebs, until I found some stairs leading to the second floor.

The warehouse had a few signs of squatters—an old shirt and some food cans and wrappers—but it looked like nobody had been there for a while. The dust on the floor was testimony to that. Unfortunately, my boots left a clear trail of my path through the building, but that was how it'd have to be. On the second floor, several windows were broken out. I found one intact and saw that by peering down I had a great view of the front door and garage of the candy company. I looked across the street to see if any lights where on in the second level of the warehouse, but couldn't see inside.

I smoked a few cigarettes and sipped on the coffee I'd brought.

Around 6:45, I heard my car engine start and smiled. I

peeked out and watched as Ricky carefully backed out of his driveway and drove slowly down the street headed west.

At seven on the dot, a car pulled up in front of the candy factory and parked. It was a rust red Lincoln Continental. A balding man, with a paunch stretching out his striped dress shirt, emerged from the car and headed straight for the front door. He unlocked it and then did something odd. Before turning the doorknob and entering, he looked around in all directions. I shrank back into the shadows even though he didn't bother to look up.

It might have been normal, cautious behavior born of running a business in a semi-dangerous part of town. But then wouldn't he have scanned the neighborhood before getting out of his car? His behavior was suspicious to me.

A few seconds later, he'd slipped into the building and closed the door behind him. I waited.

Within a few minutes, lights flickered on in the upper-story windows of the building.

I couldn't see inside even when I used the binoculars I'd brought in my small backpack.

I slumped back down to a sitting position. King wanted me here. But why?

If it wasn't the building, what was it?

At eight, about a dozen people arrived at the building and lined up to file inside—the employees.

I was already sick of trying to figure out why I was there. I'd go ask.

The line moved slowly. I was the last one waiting to go inside. The guy in front of me gave me a surprised glance at first, but then turned and ignored me, talking to the woman in front of him in Spanish about the football game the night before.

When I reached the door, I saw the pudgy man standing just inside, filing time cards into a slot on the wall. He looked up in time for me to stick my gun under his chin. His eyes were blood-shot, and his nose was large and red. His eyes kept flickering down to something on the ground. I looked down to make sure it wasn't a gun. It was a paper bag with a bottle of booze poking out.

The workers had already disappeared somewhere inside the building.

"Let's talk," I said.

His eyes were wide with fear.

"You're her?"

"What?" His words startled me. I kept the muzzle of my gun pressed tightly to his jaw.

"I've got a message for you. From the guy with white hair."

My heart raced double time. I narrowed my eyes. "Spit it out, then."

"He says you're too late."

I thrust the gun harder into his flesh.

"What are you talking about?"

"I'm just the messenger. I swear."

"How do you know King?"

"That's his name?"

I didn't have time for games. I yanked his head back and jammed the gun into the fleshy spot under the mandible. "Answer my question."

He had a hard time talking with his chin jutting up in the air from my gun, but I didn't care. He still had a tongue, right? Until I heard differently, I had to assume he was colluding with King.

"He just came by one day and told me if I knew what was good for me I'd pass on that message to you." I heard the trickle of water. The poor son-of-bitch was pissing himself.

I put my gun back in its holster.

The man sagged in relief, nearly collapsing onto a stool near the door.

"When was this?"

"Two days ago."

That made sense.

"What was he driving?"

The man frowned, remembering. "He got into the back of a black car."

I nodded.

"How did you know I was the one he mentioned."

"He showed me a picture."

I drew back. "What?"

"It was a picture of you."

"Describe it. Exactly."

"You were walking down a sidewalk. With some black man, or excuse me, African-American man."

James.

"Where was it?"

"I don't know. I didn't recognize the area, but it looked like a place with a bunch of restaurants."

"What else do you remember about it?"

"You were smiling and holding this guy's hand."

"What'd the guy look like?"

"Black guy. Built. Sharp dresser." Yep. James.

"What else?"

The man looked away.

"Answer me or I get out my gun again."

"He was in the picture, too."

I raised an eyebrow.

"The guy with white hair."

My heart flew up into my throat.

"He was way back of you two. Like he was following you."

I swallowed. Jesus Christ.

"Do you remember what I was wearing?"

"Yeah. Because ..." He paused.

"Just say it."

"Well, I don't know anyone who wears leather pants."

Leather Pants. It must've been a few months ago in the spring when the weather was cooler. I hadn't worn my leather pants since then and had only recently thought about digging them out of my closet again.

I yanked one of the time cards out of the filing system on the wall, grabbed a pen off the counter and scribbled my number on it. "This is my number. If you can think of anything else or if he shows up again, use it." I stuck the card in his shirt pocket. "Got it?"

He nodded emphatically.

"You can have your morning drink now." I let the door slam behind me.

Motherfucker. King had been stalking me for months. And James.

Before I'd made it across the street, I'd dialed his number.

"Hey baby," he said, and I was flooded with relief.

"Hi."

"What's up?"

"When do you get off?" I asked.

"Not until four."

"I need to see you."

13

THE KID BROUGHT MY CAR BACK IN ONE PIECE. I WAS SITTING ON his porch eating sunflower seeds with his mom when he pulled up. Her eyes practically popped out of her head. She stood, wiping her hands on her jeans and squinting to see the car better.

"That's yours?"

"Yup." I'd told her I'd loaned him my car for the day to thank him for helping my niece at school when some guy was picking on her. It was a little white lie, but the mother puffed up in pride when I said it, so I figured it was worth it.

Mom worked from four in the morning to one in the afternoon loading UPS trucks and then would start her second job waiting tables from three to ten. She was a badass. We got along just fine.

She told me a lot about Ricky. The kid had potential. A lot of it. She worked two jobs to pay for his private school. Said it was worth it.

Now she stood, brushing her hands off on her black slacks. "You trusted my boy with that car?"

I had a mouthful of sunflower seeds, so I just nodded emphatically.

She let out a low whistle.

"He's a good kid," I said.

She sighed and turned toward me. "I know."

While we'd sat there, she'd told me how his older brother had taken off years ago to become a gangbanger, and her greatest fear was that her younger son would follow in his footsteps. His brother was already sniffing around, showing up in expensive cars and flashing fancy jewelry and cash. His mom was worried Ricky would take the same path.

I felt a little sick. Had I given him a taste of the rich things by letting him take my car? My kindness might have backfired. Fuck.

Ricky walked up to the porch, blushing. "Hey, mama."

She tousled his hair. "You got a new friend, I see."

"Sorry I didn't tell you." He looked down.

She clucked a little and then headed toward the door. "I've got to get ready for work." She nodded at me. "Pleased to meet you."

"Likewise."

Ricky handed me the keys. "Thanks."

"How'd it go?"

He grinned. "It was funny."

I laughed. "I bet."

He shoved his hands in his pocket.

Stepping off the porch, I turned. "Hey, listen. You're a smart kid. Your mama told me you're in all sorts of AP classes and that you might even be able to go to college early. You want a car like that? You have the brains to figure out how to get one the right way."

A scowl appeared on his face.

I understood. I'd turned from a friend to a parental figure. But I had to say it.

"Listen. You have my number. If things get crazy around here, you call me, okay?"

He bit his lip.

I raised my eyebrow. "Okay?"

He nodded. But I didn't believe him. And that worried me.

I made a note to come visit him next month. See what was up.

———

WHEN JAMES WALKED into the loft I raced over and grabbed him in a hug and then lifted my head and kissed him until we were both sputtering for air.

"Guess you missed me?" He said when I finally pulled away.

I led him by the hand over to the café table. "I've got some things to tell you."

I came clean and told him everything I'd done, including the B&E at the rehab house, and what I'd learned, especially about the photo with King following us.

"It's a warning," I said. "He wanted me to know about the photo. He's threatening you. He was stalking us."

James frowned. "He's been in town this whole time?"

"At least since spring as far as I can figure."

James shook his head. "He's setting you up. He wants you afraid. All this is part of his game. He wants you off-guard and off-kilter."

"I know."

"Don't let him win."

I stood up and paced. "I want him dead, James. Honestly."

"Jesus Christ, Gia," he said and shook his head. "I'm a cop.

You can't say those things to me. What if he ends up dead? Then you're a suspect."

"*James.*" My voice held a warning.

"I know. I know. But don't say those things to me."

A wave of sadness washed over me. That's why it would never work with us. It couldn't. And now, just dating me put him in danger. In the sights of a madman. A killer. A *racist* killer who would like nothing more than to get rid of my boyfriend.

The thought sent fury raging through me. "God damn it. Damn him."

I kicked the wall. I grabbed my backpack and took off toward the door. "I'm going to the Dojo. If I don't do something physical, I'm going to explode."

James didn't try to stop me. His eyes met mine for a few seconds and then he gave the slightest nod, releasing me.

I stormed down the stairs, swearing under my breath.

When I stepped onto the sidewalk, I paused and glanced around out of habit and felt for the gun in my back waistband. As my fingers touched the cool metal of the grip, I wished with all my being that King would step out of the shadows so I could shoot him between the eyes and end this once and for all.

14

"You seem a little tense," Kato said.

"Because I am." I stopped and grabbed a rag to wipe off the sweat that was dripping down my temples. I'd headed her the second James left my loft this morning. I needed the healing of intense physical activity to relieve my anxiety over King.

"You know Darling talked to me about you making an altar for Day of the Dead. November second is right around the corner."

I made a face. "Would you two quit ganging up on me?"

He laughed. "Was that obvious?"

"Disgustingly so."

"We just think that maybe you haven't really dealt with what happened to Bobby yet."

I threw the rag in a pile of dirty ones in the corner. "You're right. I haven't. So sue me."

"Gia..." He sounded disappointed. *Join the Disappointed-in-Gia Club*, I thought.

"Kato, how would you feel if you left a trail of blood behind you everywhere you went everyone you loved was murdered, snatched from you violently, in the worst possible ways?"

Even Kato had been attacked by someone trying to get to me.

His eyes grew sad. "I can't understand. I don't know how I would feel. I'm sorry."

"You don't have to apologize, but I don't know how to move on."

"You could at least try the *Dia de los Muertos* plan."

"It's a plan now?" I headed toward the drinking fountain.

"Maybe. I'm doing it."

That stopped me in my tracks.

"You?"

"Yeah, for my grandmother. I never got a chance to say goodbye to her. She died in New York. But we're keeping our altar at home in our living room."

"Huh." That made me think. If Kato and his hippie wife, Suzie, thought it was okay, maybe I should consider it.

"I don't think it would work for me."

"Okay," he said. "Break's over. Let's work on that kick."

"Can we do swords today?"

"Next time."

I'd been fascinated by the Sicilian art of Gladiatura Moderna ever since an encounter with my aunt, Eva. She called herself the Queen of Spades and was like this vigilante goddess in Sicily, taking from the rich and giving to the poor.

I don't know where she actually lives, but she'd given me a card with a phone number on it in case I ever got in trouble.

It was cool, but part of me wished she could just be a regular aunt to me. Maybe a woman who lived in the city and who had me over for dinner once in a while. I was lonely for family. I'd created my own family—Kato was part of it—but I also had Italian blood running through me, and deep in my DNA I yearned for a family connection.

———

AN HOUR LATER, after Kato worked me out and listened to my fears in between parries and thrusts, I was back at my loft.

My place was empty. I didn't see any sign of James or my dog. My heart leaped into my throat until I saw the door to the roof was open. Django could open it on his own. Maybe he was up there going to the bathroom.

When I poked my head up at the top of the stairs, I saw James sitting on a patio chair. Django was lying by his feet and gave me a sleepy lazy wag of his tail as a greeting. Three beer cans sat on the table beside James. He cracked open a fourth and took a long pull on it before speaking.

"I don't work tomorrow. Union rules because I worked the double."

"Best news I've heard all day," I said and tucked myself onto the patio chair beside him, putting my head on his shoulder.

He grabbed me by my hair, not roughly but enough to lift my head, and then his mouth was on mine. Soon, he'd ripped off my top and was unbuttoning my pants. We were on top of a roof in the middle of San Francisco, but I didn't care. Well, not much. I pulled him into the shadowy recesses of my grape arbor and showed him just how I felt.

In the night, I woke to find James pacing. His figure was a dark shadow passing through huge rectangles of light from the streetlights pouring through the massive loft windows.

"What's wrong?" I sat up.

"I don't know."

"What don't you know?"

He came and perched on the side of the bed and took my hand. "Every time I feel like we're making progress, like maybe there is a break through, you retreat."

I blinked. "I don't understand."

But inside I squirmed. Shortly after we'd finished making love earlier, James had mentioned something about our future together, something about maybe living together, and I'd shut down completely. I'd clammed up and rolled over with my back to him. I wasn't proud of it. It was just the way it was.

I swallowed. "You mean how I reacted about living together?"

"Yes." His voice was quiet in the dark.

I didn't know what to say to that.

He came closer, and his eyes glowed in the streetlights. "Is this going anywhere? Am I wasting my time?"

The first sentence I could deal with. The second one sent me jerking away.

"Wasting your time? You tell me?" My voice was angry.

"I don't mean to be a dick," he said. "But I need to know if this is worth investing myself in."

"I can't answer that for you." I folded my arms across my chest and scooted back against the headboard out of his reach. "You knew what you were getting into."

"I just hoped—"

"That you could change me?"

"No!" He was angry now too. But then his voice calmed. "I just hoped that maybe you could grow to trust me."

My anger waned. "James, I trust you. It's not that." I reached for his hand. "I just don't trust the world."

He didn't answer.

"I don't trust the world to not take you away from me."

"You're not over Bobby." His voice was resigned, matter-of-fact.

"I don't even know what that means?"

"Let me rephrase that. You're not over his death."

I couldn't argue. "I'm trying."

"I believe you," he said. He stood and exhaled loudly. "Gia. This isn't your problem, but I am forty years old. I want to be a young father. But I'm running out of daylight, as they say."

"That's a stupid turn of phrase."

"You know what I mean."

Again, I had nothing. I got out of bed, grabbed my robe and a pack of cigarettes, and headed to the roof. I sat in the cold smoking and wondering what the fuck James wanted from me. I wasn't even sure I *wanted* to "be over" Bobby's death. What did that even mean? It seemed a betrayal no matter how I looked at it.

When I came back downstairs, James was gone.

15

"I THINK JAMES IS LOSING PATIENCE WITH ME."

I was in the back room of Darling's salon. We were playing cribbage and drinking Jack Daniels. I needed to spill. I was worried I was about to lose James. He wasn't returning my calls. An entire day had come and gone since he left my place, angry. Earlier, I'd even gone and hid outside his apartment just to make sure he was still alive.

He could avoid answering my calls and texts if he was alive. As long as King hadn't gotten to him.

I'd nearly collapsed with relief when I saw him come flying out of his apartment building, hair still wet as he headed for his car and to his shift at the police station. But the relief was soon replaced by sadness. He must be really angry with me. I headed straight to cry on Darling's shoulder.

"You better hold on to him," she said now. "He's a good man."

"I thought you hated cops?" I eyed her suspiciously.

"He's different."

"You can say that again."

"You smell that?" She stood and sniffed in exaggeration.

"Stop."

She gestured toward the cribbage board. "Smells like someone got skunked."

"Today must be my lucky day," I said, rolling my eyes.

She laughed. "I think the whole month of October is going to be lucky for me, honey."

I looked at the calendar on her wall. It had a picture of Etta James on it. Today was TK. Halloween was coming up. So was the Day of the Dead.

I was bashful about bringing it up, but Kato's words had stuck with me.

"Darling? You said something once about making peace with Bobby's spirit on the Day of the Dead?"

"Yes?" She nailed me with those Cleopatra eyes. I shrunk back, but the wall stopped me from getting away from that penetrating gaze. "Is there a question in there somewhere?"

I shrugged. "I guess so." Wouldn't help for me to seem *too* eager. I knew Darling would gleefully drag it out all day if I revealed I was anxious for her advice or help. I stood and went to fix us another drink.

She cackled and followed me. I wasn't fooling anyone.

"You want to know or not?"

"Yes," I said, my voice filled with exasperation.

"If I tell you, you gonna call it 'creepy voodoo shit?'"

"No." My voice was low, humbled.

"You build an altar."

I couldn't help it, I felt my forehead scrunch. I didn't want to "build" anything.

"You heard me," she said. "You can have his picture and some of the stuff he loved most on this earth."

Images of Bobby—smiling at me, above me making love, just getting out of the shower—flashed before me. The memories alone felt like a stab to the heart.

"I don't think I can."

"A five-year-old can."

"I don't know," I said. I gulped most of my drink in one take.

"You know."

She was right.

For a second, I thought about making an altar for my parents. I missed them so much sometimes it hurt to breathe. But for some reason their deaths didn't hang over me like Bobby's did. Actually, I knew the reason. They hadn't died *because* of me.

Bobby? He'd died because of me.

I couldn't make peace with his death or the guilt.

Telling Darling I'd think about it, I headed to the liquor store before I changed my mind. I was going to gather everything I'd need, and it would start with the alcohol he loved the most. Besides, the liquor store was on my way home, and I was out of whiskey. It was going to be a long night alone without it.

Back at my loft, I dug around deep in my closet to unearth the box where I'd stashed some of Bobby's belongings. It was right next to my mother's hat box that contained my remembrances of her.

Most of Bobby's belongings had been packed up and sent to his parents. I wasn't even sure the box had gotten to them because I'd never heard from them. They blamed me for his death. Since I also blamed myself, I couldn't very well argue with them, could I?

Inside the box were the things that I'd kept in Bobby's memory. Slumped on the floor, tears streaming down my face, I took them out slowly, one at a time, and held them in my hands.

The box itself was significant: it'd once contained Bobby's beloved running shoes. He was a runner, something I never could understand, but respected. It was as much a part of him as his curly hair.

A ticket stub from when we went to the San Francisco Symphony's production of Schindler's List. I'll never forget looking over and seeing his eyes gleaming with unshed tears. Even a violinist on stage was weeping that night.

A dried red rose—the first rose he gave me. A Rev. Horton Heat postcard flier from when they played in Santa Cruz the night we met. A note he left me saying he'd fallen for me.

I let the tears run down my face as I carefully held and examined each item, remembering. As I wiped my face, I wondered if this—the gathering, handling, and remembrance of a loved one's objects—was part of the healing process.

Okay. I think I had enough items to make an altar. I looked at them all splayed out beside me on the floor. Django kept sniffing at them and wagging his tail and then looking at the door, and it made me cry harder. I buried my face in his fur. "You miss him too, huh, buddy?"

Now what? I got on my laptop It didn't take long to find images of different types of altars. Crap. I needed more stuff. Pictures. Duh. That should've been a given. But my heart sank at the idea of going through my pictures of Bobby right then. I was going to need another drink for that.

And I'd have to buy candles and maybe flowers. And a sugar skull. And a silver milagro.

Despite myself, I felt a surge or energy thinking about making Bobby's altar. I wouldn't go overboard. No flowers. No skulls. No milagro.

I'd keep it simple—like Bobby.

His running shoes box. Inside I'd set his love letter, the ticket stub, the dried rose, the band flier. Around the box, I'd place a few favorite photos of him. His Bourbon. (Although I had a feeling it would be stolen left out in the park.) Candles. That would be enough.

The more I looked at other altars the more I felt good about keeping it simple. I didn't need to go overboard to remember him.

One website said Day of the Dead was a 3,000-year-old ritual. How could that even be? Then I read how you needed to leave food and drink to fortify your loved one's spirit on the journey to ... wherever. Food. I'd make his favorite chocolate chip cookies for him. And a peanut butter and jelly sandwich. He was a simple guy with simple tastes. I don't know how he ever fell for someone like me—a complicated train wreck.

Then I looked up San Francisco Day of the Dead. It mentioned the procession, called the Festival of Altars. I would walk with others to Garfield Park where all the altars would be displayed. We would dress up. Music would play. It all seemed bizarre.

I could do it. I could put the altar in a corner of Garfield Park closest to my old Russian Hill apartment where we had fallen in love.

That's when I read this: "Ofrendas (offerings) encourage the dead to come back and hear the prayers of their loved ones."

That was it. Why I was doing it. I was calling Bobby's spirit back to ask his forgiveness. Oh my God. When did I start believing in this? I don't know when exactly it happened, but it did.

I was going to make an altar, and I was going to kneel in front of it on the Day of the Dead, and I was going to beg and plead and cry for Bobby to please, please, please forgive me.

Looking at my Bourbon bottle, I realized I was drunk. I needed to go to bed.

Leaving everything on the floor, I crawled under the covers and fell into a deep, nightmare-ridden sleep.

16

IN THE MORNING, THE FIRST THING I DID WAS CHECK MY PHONE.

No calls or texts from James.

He must be really pissed.

The second thing I did was reach over to my nightstand to grab the bourbon bottle. I scooched to a sitting position and chugged straight out of the bottle. Hair of the dog. I wasn't proud of it. I hadn't had to do that in months. Dating James had kept me halfway sober for the first time in years.

But screw it. I needed to be on my game today. A hangover would just get in the way. I'd only drink enough to get me up and at 'em.

As I made an espresso and spiked it with a healthy shot of bourbon, I didn't feel an ounce of guilt There were some teenage girls out there that needed my help. Nobody else seemed to give a damn about them. I mean, sure some cops on the case, like James, probably did care, but that wasn't good enough. Maybe they weren't able or willing to do what was necessary.

Django had bumped the lever opening the door to the roof and was up there probably doing his morning constitutional.

Grabbing my coffee, I headed up to greet him and the morning air.

But when I left the stairway and stepped onto the rooftop, I froze in horror.

Django was whining. And circling something bloody.

It was long and pink and bloody—a rectangle of bloody flesh slightly pointed at one end. Meat. I was surprised that Django hadn't devoured it.

That's when it struck me. It was a tenderloin cut of beef. Bile rose in my throat. How the fuck did that get on my roof? That's when I heard the sound. I looked up. A drone. I reflexively reached behind me into my waistband for my gun, but it wasn't there. I'd never needed it on my roof.

Squinting, I saw the drone had clawed legs. It had left this little alarming message for me. And now it wanted to make sure I knew it was watching.

Or rather, that *he* was watching.

It was King.

I pointed my fingers into the shape of a gun and took aim, reaching my arm out toward the drone and cocking my thumb as if I'd fired. I did this for several seconds and then put my hands on my waist, waiting.

The drone didn't budge for several minutes. The sunlight was making my eyes water, but I refused to look away.

Finally, without warning, the drone rose straight up so quickly and so high that I couldn't tell which direction it headed after that because it vanished into the blue sky.

Only then—when it had disappeared—did I shoo Django aside to take a closer look at the morbid offering left for me.

A tenderloin meant one thing. King was here. In the Tenderloin.

It was here, in a building in the Tenderloin district, where I'd had my first show down with King. Where he had marked me. Scarred my face.

That warehouse, the same one that contained the bodies of his victims and had a long, dark evil history in our city, had been demolished last year. I'd gone by there a few months ago. The rubble was confined behind a huge chain link fence. I wondered if anybody was ever going to clean it up or do something with that land. I hoped not. There were too many ghosts there.

The building was in the Forgotten Island part of the Tenderloin—so named that because it was so often shrouded in fog. Even before I knew it was King's lair, I'd always gotten a chill passing by the warehouse. And later, when I dug deeper, I'd learned it had a dark, evil history of murder.

Staring at the hunk of meat, I knew with certainty that King was trying to terrorize me.

He wanted me to be afraid, but he didn't know that fear powered me. I was energized, fired up, fervent to fight him.

I'd make a plan.

And I'd be waiting.

17

DANNY OPENED THE DOOR WITH ONE HAND. HIS OTHER HELD A folded slab of pizza.

"That smells good. You got any more?" I said as I stepped inside his apartment.

He had a mouthful of food, so he gestured toward his kitchen table.

It was piled with tiny metal bars and bolts and parts. And empty boxes. And crushed soda cans and a stack of old pizza boxes.

Off to one side was the open pizza box. The slice I grabbed from it was still warm and gooey with melted cheese. Yum.

We didn't talk until he'd shoved in yet another wedge of pie into his mouth and I'd finished two head-sized triangles of my own.

I helped myself to his fridge, leaning down and peering inside, hoping for booze to wash it down my meal, but knowing that it would be fully stocked with only diet soda.

I grabbed one, popped the top and nearly downed the whole thing before I came up for air.

"Hey, Gia," Danny said looking at me side-eyed.

"How you been?"

"Good. I got a job from that guy you put me in touch with."

"Sweet. He's a good dude."

"I only have to go into the office once a week."

"Perfect."

I'd signed papers for him to be emancipated from his messed-up family a few years ago. He was now a free agent. I'd also put him in touch with a venture capitalist who needed his hacker skills on the down low.

He was a fucking genius.

"I'm going to need to put you on my pay roll, too."

"Killer," he said, but then looked guilty. "You know you don't have to pay me. I'll help you for free."

"I know, honey. But this way I won't feel guilty calling you all hours of the day."

He was a night owl—awake all night and sleeping all day. I was surprised he'd even been up and about when I arrived today.

I told him about the drone dumping the tenderloin on my roof.

"Can you do some type of patrol? Like a cop car would do a drive-by to check on suspicious activity, but do it from the air, maybe a few times a night?"

"Sure."

"I'll want the footage recorded, but what I'm most interested is you staying out of sight and monitoring for any other drone activity. I need to know where the drone's home base is. I know you can outsmart that assclown."

"You better believe it," he said. "If he comes anywhere near your roof, I've got him."

I slapped his back and grabbed another slice of pizza before heading to the door. "I knew I could count on you."

The door handle was in my palm when he called my name. "Gia? Who exactly is trying to mess with you?"

I exhaled and felt my entire body tense. I didn't turn around.

He picked up on it immediately. "You're kidding me? He's back?"

I slipped out the door, closing it softly behind me.

Yeah. King had left quite a legacy of terror behind him.

My next stop was Darling's salon.

I came in through the front door. A few women who didn't know me raised eyebrows and exchanged looks. I'm pretty sure I'm the only white woman who ever steps foot in Darling's place, but as soon as one of the stylists I knew gave me a shout out, the tension dissipated.

"She's in the back, hon," Mona said, gesturing toward Darling's private room.

Thea came out from where she was organizing some brushes to give me a kiss on the cheek. "How've you been, Gia?"

"Just fine. How's that grandbaby?"

Thea's face lit up. "Just the cutest thing ever."

"I bet."

"Thanks for the book. I read it to him the other day, and I swear he smiled. They say they don't smile that young, but I know he did."

"That book's my favorite." I gave everyone I knew the same book when a baby was born into their family: Sandra Boynton's *"Snuggle Puppy."*

After catching up with Thea's daughter's postpartum struggles as a new mother, I headed to the big steel-reinforced door that led to Darling's inner chamber.

I pushed a button and the security camera in the corner flickered to life. A second later, the door emitted a clicking sound, and I pushed it open.

Darling was sitting at her massive oak desk with reading

glasses pushed up on her nose. She smiled and stood, stretching.

"Oh good. I need a break. Damn taxes are killing me."

"Good thing you only file them on your legal ventures, or you'd really be hurting," I said.

"Hush now." She looked around furtively.

"What? You think this place is bugged?"

She shrugged. "You never know. The more money I make, the more enemies I seem to get."

"That sucks," I said, flinging myself onto the couch and reaching for a joint out of a nice bowl full of them on the coffee table. I offered her the bowl, and she made a face. She didn't smoke. And she was even threatening to give up drinking, which horrified me.

"I always like your company, but I'm really glad you came by today," she said, pouring us shots of Jack Daniels. "I got those mommas calling me wanting to know what I'm doing to find their baby girls. They are coming over later after they get off work for an update. What am I supposed to tell them, Gia?"

I inhaled deeply, held it for several seconds, and exhaled. "This is good stuff."

"Only the best for my guests."

She handed me my drink and sat down beside me. She kicked off her heels, and put her feet up on the coffee table. She used a small remote to turn on some jazz. We both sat there contentedly for a few minutes. I stubbed out the joint after only a few puffs. I needed my wits about me.

"Darling, we got to make a plan."

"Sugar, I've always got a plan."

"True story."

Darling hadn't built her two empires—the thriving salon and her underground venture providing false documents—by not having a plan.

I filled her in on everything I'd learned since I last saw her.

"That's not the news I was hoping to hear," she said, shaking her head.

"I know." I felt suitably scolded. I'd hoped to know more by now. In fact, I'd hoped to have found those girls already and stopped King for good.

"Hey," I said eagerly to change the subject.

"Yes?"

"I bought some stuff."

"Can you please be more specific?" She raised an eyebrow in irritation.

"Altar stuff."

She tilted her head and this time raised both eyebrows. "Really?"

"Yep. I'm going to do it."

A smile spread across her face, and she stood, patting my knee as she passed.

"Good girl."

18

I'll admit, I'm not proud of it, but after I left Darling's place, I hired a car and staked out the back lot of the police station. I needed to make sure James was safe and that King hadn't gotten to him.

Since James wouldn't return my calls, stalking was in order. It had been three days since he stormed out.

"Turn that up," I said to the driver, gesturing to the radio.

He smiled, and his one gold tooth reflected the fading sunlight. "You like Eminem?"

"Not really. Only this song." It was a lie. I liked everything Eminem put out. Why did I always feel the need to be difficult? God only knew.

James once said I was like a prickly pear. I never really thought about it. What did that mean? I think he just meant I was sometimes a pain in the ass.

"I've never sat on a police station before."

The way he phrased it made me pause. He turned his head, and that's when I saw it. Prison tattoo. Poking out from the collar of his shirt. Ex-con.

"What sort of establishments *have* you sat on?" I said in a teasing voice. Bank. Convenience store. Drug dealer's house. What *was* he? The fucking getaway driver?

He shifted and stroked his jaw. Unconscious tell. He was uncomfortable AF.

I'd nailed him.

Clearing my throat, I leaned forward and said into his ear. "Because if you have some certifiable driving skills, I might need you more often."

He didn't turn. I watched his Adam's apple bob. Oh, how cute, little old me was making him nervous. And he didn't even know I was carrying. The gun in my waistband was digging into my back. I'd have to start wearing my holster all the time now that I knew King was back in town.

"So?" I left my question hanging.

I could almost see the struggle going on inside him. He knew I had money. I'd paid him $300 cash when I got in to his car, telling him it could be thirty minutes or it could be three hours.

Finally, the dude with the white wings on his shoulder won the internal battle and he said, "I promised my old lady I'd stay away from that shit. I'm on probation."

"Oh, don't worry. Your old lady won't have any problems with what I'm doing. I'm cleaning up the streets. You know? The only ones who won't like what I do are the really bad dudes, you know the ones that do stuff to kids?"

"Yeah, fuck them," he said, raising his voice. "I got grandkids now, and I'd do anything to keep them safe."

"That's right. Me and you. We're talking the same language, my friend," I said. I patted him on the shoulder and sat back.

He didn't seem convinced. He met my eyes in the rearview mirror. "Then why we staking out the cops?"

"Long story."

He raised an eyebrow.

I waited him out.

"I don't like this. Either you tell me why we're here or you can have your damn money back."

I'd really made him nervous.

But I really liked him and needed a good driver on speed dial for situations like this. I glanced at all his personal info again on the app on my phone and took a screenshot of it. His name was Tony. He had good reviews.

"I'm serious," he said and tried to hand me the money.

I waved the money away.

"I'll tell you why we're here ..."

Just then, James walked out of the back door in plain clothes. He was walking across the parking lot toward his car. Tony followed my gaze.

"Dude you're waiting for?"

"My guy."

He jutted his chin. "That cop?"

I nodded.

"So, why we here again?"

I smiled at Tony. "Making sure my boyfriend didn't get himself killed."

———

AFTER TONY DROPPED me back off at my place, I tried calling James. He didn't answer, so I tapped his number again. Straight to voice mail this time.

So, I texted him.

"Please answer."

Nothing.

So, I texted him again.

"Please answer."

Finally, after I sent the tenth text my phone rang.

"This better be an emergency."

"Sorry, I was worried."

"I needed a break from you."

"Needed?" I asked.

"Need."

My heart sunk. I felt tears spring to my eyes. I was grateful he couldn't see me.

"For how long?" My voice was meek.

He sighed loudly. "Just a few days."

"It's been a few days." I hated that my voice sounded whiny. "I'm worried about you. Because of King."

"I'm a cop, Gia. I can handle myself."

I remained silent.

"I'm being careful," he added.

I swallowed. "You promise?"

"Yes."

19

I SAT BOLT UPRIGHT IN THE DARK, HEART POUNDING, FROZEN IN THE night, straining to hear what had woken me. There was a strange buzzing sound in my loft that I didn't recognize and couldn't quite place.

As my eyes adjusted, I saw a lighter square of darkness indicating the door to the roof was showing it was open. Django didn't usually make middle-of-the-night visits to relieve himself, but it wasn't completely unheard of, either.

For a second I relaxed. But the buzzing remained consistent, like a muffled chain saw or mammoth mosquito. And it wasn't filtering in from the open doorway, it was *inside* my loft.

I swore and lunged for the gun under my pillow.

That's when I saw the blinking red and green lights in the corner by the ceiling. Jesus!

The goddamn drone was back. And was in my loft, hovering near a tall corner of my ceiling, watching me. Where the hell was Django? He should be barking or doing something. Fear sucked all the moisture out of my throat.

I whistled for him but didn't hear him padding down the stairs from the roof. My face felt icy with fear for him.

Taking aim, I pointed the gun at the drone. I'd shoot the fucker out of the sky. But it immediately zipped across the room toward me. I lowered my gun. I remembered my instructions to Danny. If I shot the drone, then he wouldn't be able to track it back to where the operator was located. And that's what I was after—King's location.

It hovered about ten feet away from my bed, which was also directly across from the open door to the roof. It must have night vision. Frankly, the thing was giving me the creeps. It looked like a big bug watching me. And I was getting increasingly nervous that Django hadn't stormed down the stairs to attack it. If anything happened to my dog, I swear I would leave a trail of blood from here to Los Angeles.

I whistled again. Nothing.

I raised the gun again and the drone jolted toward the door, but then stopped when I didn't fire. I knew if my aim was accurate, I could take it out. There was no way it could possibly dodge my bullet. The fastest drone went about forty miles-per-hour, a lot slower than my 1,700 miles-per-hour bullet. But I didn't really want to shoot it down. At least not yet.

I slowly walked toward where it was hovering by the door to the roof. I'd shoot it if it got in my way. I needed to find Django. I was nearly underneath it when it took off out the door at lightning speed.

I chased it up onto the rooftop in the tee-shirt and underwear I'd slept in. As I emerged onto the rooftop, blinking in the bright morning light, I saw it zip straight up and then out of sight right before I saw Django's limp form under the grape arbor.

I raced to him and dropped to my knees, reached for his neck, and tried to find a pulse.

"Django!" I sobbed the word. I couldn't feel a thing. I reached down to his belly, hoping to feel a heartbeat there. I placed my palm on his belly and then nearly cried in relief when I felt the movement of his breathing.

I buried my face in the fur around his neck and whispered into his ear. "Hang in there, buddy. I'm getting help."

I kissed his nose and then raced down the stairs. Once in my loft, I looked around wildly until I saw my phone on the table and lunged for it.

———

"I'M glad you brought him in," the veterinarian said. I'd rushed in while I it was still dark, barely able to carry Django's limp body.

I'd shot up from my chair in the emergency room lobby when he came out the double doors. Without my dog. "Is he okay?"

"We induced vomiting. Apparently, he'd eaten some raisins." I knew that raisins could be toxic to dogs.

"Is he okay?"

"We're going to want to keep him hooked up to an IV overnight, and then do some blood work in the morning to check his blood liver levels."

I scrunched my face. My phone buzzed in my back pocket, but I didn't take my eyes off the doctor.

"I don't understand."

The doctor chewed his inner lip before answering, which sent terror streaking through me.

"It's too soon to tell. He's a very sick dog. Raisins alone are toxic and it looks like they were dipped in a solution that knocked him out. We think that he should, under the best-case scenario, wake up within an hour or two."

The news made me sick. My phone buzzed again and I ignored it.

"He's still out? And you induced vomiting?"

"He's in a drowsy state. As soon as he vomited, he fell back under."

"Oh my God."

"We can call you when he wakes up. But we're definitely going to want to monitor him overnight."

"I'll wait here." I crossed my arms and met the doctor's eyes.

"I understand completely. We will let you know when anything changes."

"Thank you."

After he left, I sank into the couch in the lobby, staring at the vending machine and coffee maker as my stomach grumbled. But I was too upset to eat or drink anything.

I reached behind me and took out my phone. A message from Danny. I called him back immediately.

"Got him," he said when he answered.

"Oh, thank God. Because as soon as my dog is okay I'm going over there and killing someone."

There was silence on the other end.

"The drone dropped poison on my roof. They poisoned my dog."

"Oh no." He sounded genuinely upset and it made me want to cry.

"He might not make it." Now I had tears streaming down my face.

Danny cleared his throat.

"Can I come be with you? Wherever you are? I can come there." He sounded awkward and sweet and it made me cry harder.

"No, it's okay," I said. "But thanks." I paused. "That means a lot."

After we hung up, I used my shirt sleeve to wipe away my tears.

Rage surged through me.

King was a dead man.

20

DJANGO WOKE UP THREE AGONIZING HOURS LATER.

I'd jumped to my feet when the doctor came out and then sagged in relief when he smiled.

"He's awake."

"Can I see him?"

The doctor frowned. "He's in our surgical unit. He's sedated through his IV so we can keep the fluids and antibiotics moving through him. But it's a light sedation. I don't want him to struggle. I'd rather he relaxes for a while."

I swallowed. I wanted to insist on seeing my dog, but I didn't want to disturb him, either.

Fighting against all my instincts, I nodded.

"The next steps are for us to keep monitoring him, keep him on the IV, and then check his blood work tomorrow morning. Why don't you head home? We'll call if anything changes, but he's doing great and he's in the right place."

I looked around. A woman at the receptionist desk was also shrugging on a jacket and hoisting a purse strap onto her shoulder.

There was nothing for me to do here.

I left and headed straight to Danny's.

A couple heads poked out his apartment building windows when I pulled up. My Ferrari was obnoxious like that. I'd already decided in Oakland that I probably needed a lower-profile form of transportation. And because I thought it was stupid for someone to own more than one vehicle, that meant selling this baby. My heart clenched a little at the thought, and memories of racing up the coast toward wine country would haunt me, but it was the right thing to do.

Danny stuck his head out his window, too. I looked up as I got out of my car and responded to his questioning look with a thumbs up.

It was more optimism than I felt.

―――――

"THE DRONE IS a DXL Dissenter Pro and is only twenty decibels loud. It can reach speeds of fifty miles per hour, making it the fastest drone out there, but my baby was able to keep up," Danny grinned in pride. He was a big boy. Enormous. He wore jeans and a flannel shirt over a faded Green Day T-shirt. It was, quite possibly, the same outfit he'd worn the day I met him. Fashion wasn't his thing. Hacking and drones were.

"Twenty decibels?" I walked toward the window and peered out as he spoke. That meant nothing to me.

"It's a really quiet drone."

"Where'd it come from?"

He reeled off an address not far away in the Tenderloin. That made sense. King had set up shop here before. And he'd basically told me he was here by leaving that slab of meat on my roof.

I stared at the foot traffic on the sidewalk below. A homeless guy I recognized stopped pushing his cart to lean over and peer into the windows of my Ferrari. Then he straightened and looked all around and then up. When he saw me, he scowled. I blew him a kiss. I was 99 percent sure his name was Doug.

I'd tried to talk him into moving into Ethel's Place a few times, but he told me he liked living on the streets. Nobody told him what to do. I had to respect that. But I also knew the dude was a thief. He broke into cars and then sold what he found to some fence. He kept himself supplied with opioids that way.

I started toward the door. I had a few questions for Doug.

"Did it see you following it?" I said as I passed Danny, who was now sitting at his desk deep into some weird lines scrolling across several screens. He had five computers set up. I didn't know what he was doing, and I didn't need to know.

He shook his head. "No way. I'm too good."

I patted his arm and headed for the door. "I know. That's why I pay you the big bucks."

The homeless guy with the cart was nearly on the next block when I caught up to him.

"Doug?"

His eyes narrowed. "What do you want?"

I held out a twenty. "Just a question."

He chewed on his lip. "What?"

"You see a guy with white hair around the Tenderloin recently."

At first, he shook his head. "No."

I took out another twenty.

"I saw a guy. He was over by that old building they tore down."

King. For sure. The rubble of his former headquarters.

"I'll give you twenty more if you tell me what he was doing."

He looked around warily. "I saw him give a guy some Oxy."

"He was *giving* it out?"

"This other guy. Stays over at a place on Ada Avenue."

Bingo. The same street where Danny had followed King's drone with his own drone.

I put the money in Doug's shirt pocket. "You see him again, you let Danny know. That window you saw me in? That's his place. I pay for good information on the white-haired man. You can spread the word on the streets."

He turned and left without answering.

21

I DROVE STRAIGHT TO THE ADDRESS THAT DANNY HAD GIVEN ME.

It was a short squat building, only about five stories high. All the doors and windows on the first floor were boarded up. Typical Tenderloin building. Although, over the past year developers were swarming the T.L. and snatching up these buildings trying to gentrify us. But Darling made sure that anyone buying in the Tenderloin wasn't here to force out the working people. They had to prove they were making the neighborhood safer but that it would still be affordable.

This building had a For Sale sign on it.

I circled it looking for a way in. There wasn't a garage door. The other three sides of the building—those not facing the street—were surrounded by a fence, so I couldn't even go and tug on the plywood to see if it was just a prop. At least not right then when people were milling the streets surrounding it.

I'd have to come back at night.

My phone rang. It was my neighbor Thanh-Thanh. She often took Django on walks for me. I think Thanh-Thanh loved my dog as much as I did—if that were even possible.

"Where's Django? Is he with you? I wanted to walk him." She must have gone upstairs and let herself in.

I filled her in and then hung up telling her I'd keep her posted. After I parked my car in the garage, instead of taking my private elevator up to my loft, I went out the door to the street.

I was restless. And my loft seemed suddenly depressing. It would be awfully quiet without my dog. I didn't like the thought.

How could I possibly sit still when Django might be so sick?

I was about to dial Dante but then remembered he was in Cuba. I wanted so badly to call James, but I was trying to comply and let him have his space. Darling was supposedly down in San Jose all day at a family baby shower.

Staring at my phone I didn't know who to call. I obviously needed more friends.

I walked aimlessly, pausing for a second as I passed the liquor store. I wanted booze, but it wasn't even noon. But I needed to stay sharp. King was around. He was taunting me.

What I really needed to do was find where they had taken those girls.

It was time to investigate Dr. Stephen Moore. I remembered the Dragon Lady had said the rehab house was their newest facility and that they had two of them. A search on my phone yielded a listing for an office in Daly City, just south of San Francisco.

Since my motorcycle was totaled, I got the Ferrari back out of the garage and headed straight over to San Fran Ferrari. It was on the way.

The head of the dealership was so happy to buy my car off of me, he drove me to Moto San Fran in his own personal vehicle —a swanky Jaguar.

I walked out of the motorcycle dealership ten minutes later as the proud owner of a Honda Blackbird. Low-profile AF. What sold me was the black low-profile looks and the fact that it went

Day of the Dead

0-60 in 2.8 seconds. I'd walked in hoping to replace my old Ninja with an exact replica, but they'd have had to order it, and I needed a bike asap.

My Kawasaki Ninja had been able to reach speeds of 222 mph — while the Blackbird topped out at about 190, but let's face it, on city streets, when the hell would I need that extra speed? Not often enough to worry. Not when they had the Blackbird in stock.

Zooming down the 280 freeway, I reached Daly City in ten minutes instead of the normal twenty. That worked for me.

I drove straight into the parking lot of the doctor's office. I had nothing to hide. Carrying my new helmet under my arm, I checked out the exterior of the building. Looked normal enough. It was a squat orange building that stretched back quite a ways into rows of Cypress trees. The only thing that struck me as odd about the place was that there were no windows on the front of the building. Zippo. Zero. Nada.

Inside, the lobby was empty except for a young woman at the receptionist desk. She looked startled to see me. I wondered if she'd been warned about me or if they just weren't used to people dropping by.

"Is Dr. Moore in?"

Her eyes widened. "Do you have an appointment?"

So, he actually *wasn't* out of the country now was he?

"Yes." I lied smoothly.

The crease between her brows grew larger. She tapped her fingers on a keyboard and then looked up at me, frowning.

"I don't seem to have you down."

"Oh, it was personal." I lifted an eyebrow and smiled as if I had a naughty secret.

"Oh!" She couldn't hide her surprise.

"Just be a dear and tell him Gia is here."

"Last name?"

"Gia will do."

The girl looked uncertain, but I inwardly cheered as she reached for the phone.

"Dr. Moore? Gia is here."

I could hear a man's voice filtering through the handset but couldn't make out what he was saying.

It was a test. If he came out, that meant King had warned him about me. If he didn't, then he might just be an innocent pawn.

The girl hung up the phone.

"He'll be right out."

Guilty.

I winked at the receptionist and she looked away.

The "right out" turned into twenty minutes. By then, I'd memorized the lobby and its contents. Small end tables held magazines on parenting, psychology, and home making. A small, framed certificate showed Dr. Moore was a trained psychologist who specialized in teenage girls. Yup. Knew that.

When the door to the back rooms opened and Dr. Moore came out, he looked flustered—as if he'd just run a marathon to get here. His hair was disheveled, and his cheeks were flushed. He wore a white lab coat over light gray pants that matched his gray hair.

He was holding the door open for me. "Please come on back."

Score. I was dying to see what was behind the lobby door. Unfortunately, it was simply a hallway with a number of closed doors. He led me to one toward the back and gestured for me to go inside.

Off to one side of the large desk was a window revealing an inner courtyard filled with ferns and palms and fountains. "That's lovely," I said.

Dr. Moore sat in a big, black leather chair on the door side of his desk and gestured for me to sit in the matching one facing the window.

"Yes, I want my patients to look at something beautiful while we talk. They often are coming from really ugly situations, and I've found that the view relaxes them."

I nodded.

After he finished speaking, he sat there watching me. He was so still that I couldn't help myself and squirmed under his gaze. I swallowed and began.

"Glad to see you made it back into the country safely—and earlier than you'd planned. I guess we can cancel our appointment for November second. And you knew who I was right away, didn't you?"

He exhaled softly. "I'd been told you might contact me."

"By who?" I tilted my head and watched him carefully as he answered. I'd read a book by an FBI agent on how to tell if someone was lying. And despite what everyone believed, liars—at least proficient ones—never looked away when they were lying. In fact, they made more eye contact than normal to try to convince the listener that they were sincere.

Determining whether someone was lying boiled down to looking for signs that they were uncomfortable. Sometimes hard to tell with a perfect stranger. But I was watching for them.

"One of our investors." Truth.

"What is the investor's name?"

"That's an odd question." Delay tactic. Check.

"Is it?"

He shifted, slightly turning his body away from me. Check.

"We don't share investor information. I'm sure you can understand that." Truth.

"I'd understand that—if I were a patient. But clearly your investor knows me, so that should change things a little, wouldn't you think?" I smiled.

"Not really." Truth.

"Okay, here's the deal, doctor," I said. "I'm here looking into some really bad shit that's going on..." I paused.

He blanched. Good. Check.

"And right now, I'm trying to figure out just how involved you are."

A flush crept up his neck. He adjusted his tie under his lab coat. Check. Dude was getting really uncomfortable now.

"What I need from you is information on your little rehab house in Bernal Heights. You know, the one on Tompkins?"

"I don't have a facility on Tompkins." Truth.

"Not anymore. You're right. You guys cleared out. I need to know where those girls are now."

"The only rehabilitation facility we have is in the back."

"Here?"

He nodded

"You wouldn't mind if I took a look, would you?"

"Impossible. Our policy is strict privacy for our subjects." Check.

Subjects. He was truly rattled.

"I thought they were patients," I said.

He opened his mouth to answer when the receptionist burst in the door. "Doctor? The call you were waiting for?"

He jumped up. "If you'll excuse me." He headed toward his desk. I stayed put.

The receptionist looked dismayed. He sighed. "Put the call through." She left, the door slamming behind her. A moment later the desk phone rang.

"Yes. I have Gia Santella in my office right now."

He knew my last name, as well. Good to know. And he was alerting the caller that I was listening in.

"Right now?" He asked. He waited and then said, "She wants to view our facility. The inner rooms."

He listened for a minute and then his eyes shot over to the window. I followed his gaze but didn't see anything other than the foliage that was there earlier.

"I see. Okay." I swore I saw a flitter of fear cross his face.

He hung up the phone with his back to me. When he turned, he'd developed a nervous tic. His lip was twitching oddly.

I went full alert. What the hell?

"I've been granted permission to show you the facility.

My eyebrows raised practically to my hairline.

"Please follow me."

"Right now?" I stood.

"Yes."

A wave apprehension zinged through me. But I plastered a smile on my face. "Fantastic." As we stepped into the hall, I headed toward a bathroom we had passed.

"Let me just use the restroom for a second."

"Um," he said and tried to step in front of me. "I don't think... Well, we have to go right now."

I slid around his body. "I'm sure you can understand. Female stuff."

Inside the bathroom, I locked the door, turned on the faucet full bore and grabbed my cell phone. Shit. One bar. Then it disappeared. I held the phone up and got the bar back.

This was bad.

Quickly, I texted James. Just the address.

There was a knock on the door.

"Just a minute," I said.

I watched as the blue line at the top of my screen that showed the message was sending stopped halfway.

Another knock. This time more like a pounding.

"Be right there."

I closed the toilet lid and stood on the toilet reaching my arm toward what I figured was the outside of the building trying to get a better signal. The little blue line showing the text was sending was still there. Not moving. But still there.

That's when I heard her. The Dragon Lady's distinctive voice.

"I have a key, step aside."

I was out of time. I jumped off the toilet seat and jammed my phone into my back pocket under my jacket.

The door popped open, revealing the Dragon Lady. Behind her stood King.

Despite my best efforts, all the moisture was sucked from my mouth when King's eyes locked on me. There was something so disconcerting about his gaze. I couldn't put my finger on it, but it sent a wave of terror through me.

I was cornered. I readied my stance, spread my legs apart, put my hands in front of me.

They might be able to take me, but I was gonna put up a hell of a fight.

That's when the Dragon Lady lifted an odd-looking gun and fired. The stinging pain in my leg nearly dropped me. I glanced down at the dart sticking out of my thigh just as an overwhelming urge to sleep overcame me.

22

I WOKE TO DARKNESS. I TRIED TO SIT UP AND REALIZED MY ARMS and legs were strapped to the bed. I lifted my head, arching my neck and straining to see in the dark. I could make out a few shadows that were darker than the rest of the room and then after a few seconds, I saw a sliver of light on the floor shining in under the door.

The tranquilizer dart had left my thigh sore, but I couldn't reach down to it. I wondered how long I'd been out.

Lying my head back down I took an inventory of my body, starting at my scalp and scanning down, doing some deep breathing at the same time to calm my racing heart. I needed my senses sharp and clear.

My head was a bit fuzzy but was quickly clearing. My mouth was dry and my tongue felt like sandpaper moving around inside it. As I scanned my body, I could feel how tight my chest was so I tried to relax and concentrate on my breathing. My heart pounded but after taking a few seconds to regulate my breathing, it also slowed. When my scan reached my thigh, the pain where the dart had entered was minor, just a dull throbbing. All good so far.

Once I was done with my internal scan, I moved my arms and legs to try to determine how I was being restrained. My arms were held down at my side by straps at my wrist pulled tightly to the bed. I couldn't even lift them an inch. My ankles were the same.

Another band stretched across my chest, and one held down my upper thighs. Yeah, I wasn't going anywhere.

My only weapon was my head. My forehead. My teeth maybe. My chin or jaw. But that would involve someone getting extremely close to me.

I'd make it happen.

Then all of my resolve and fight seeped out of me when I remembered one thing: Django.

Panic coursed through me. I wouldn't know if he was going to live or die. I wouldn't be able to take him home if he was okay. He'd be scared and confused.

A surge of adrenaline had me straining again at the straps. I needed to get out of there and see my dog. I was desperate. Sweat dripped down my temples from my exertion. I needed a plan. I needed to escape.

For a second, I considered feigning sleep when someone walked in, letting them lean down to look at me up close and wham-o. But after what felt like eternity, I decided to speed things along and let them know I was awake. I couldn't wait any longer.

"King!" I shouted, then waited. I didn't hear a sound.

"King!"

Nothing.

"Hello?"

The door cracked, letting a bar of light into the room. It fell on my face, and I blinked furiously, willing my eyes to adjust.

A dark silhouette stood in the doorway. I couldn't make out if it was male or female.

Then the lights flickered on, momentarily blinding me and causing me to shut my eyes. When I opened them again, King stood over me. He held up my phone. I realized I was holding my breath. He'd have seen I texted James from the bathroom. Had I put his life in danger?

"Too bad your text didn't go through. We use the same technology as the feds here to block cell phone service. No message made it out of here."

The image of the blue line on my phone going nowhere popped into my head. My heart sank. Nobody knew I was here. Nobody was going to come rescue me.

As those thoughts flashed across my mind, I gritted my teeth. Nobody *needed* to come rescue me. I'd vowed a long time ago to be the type of woman that *didn't need* rescuing.

The Dragon Lady appeared beside him.

"Is she ready?"

King nodded.

"Hey, I'm here, too. Quit talking like I'm not in the room."

They both ignored me. They turned their backs and were busy at a counter. I strained my neck to see. It looked like any other exam room at a medical clinic. There was a glass jar of cotton balls. A rectangular plastic box on the wall for needle disposal. A sink.

Their bodies parted, and they turned back toward me.

Dragon Lady held a hypodermic needle.

"Wait," I said. "I don't need to be drugged. I'll talk to you. What do you want?"

I couldn't hide the panic in my voice. If they drugged me, I was essentially helpless. I'd do or say anything to avoid that and give myself a fighting chance.

"This is not punishment," King said.

The Dragon Lady smiled. "In fact, most people consider it pleasure."

Good God. What were they going to give me?

She handed King the needle and wound a rubber tourniquet around my upper arm.

"What do you want?" If I could just get the Dragon Lady to lean in some, I'd head butt her.

He tilted his head as if considering my question. Then he pursed his lips together.

"I want to create a drug that instantly stops opiate addiction," he said.

"Why?" I said and narrowed my eyes. This fucker had never wanted to help another person in his life.

"It will be worth millions of dollars," he said, raising an eyebrow as if daring me to doubt him.

"That's it? You want money?"

"And prestige. I want to be on the cover of Time magazine as Person of the Year."

"You're a wanted man."

He shrugged. "Everyone can be bought. All the way up to the president."

"I believe that," I said.

Dragon lady finished typing the rubber tourniquet around my upper arm.

"Ready," she said.

King leaned over me with the hypodermic needle.

"We are so close," he said. His eyes bored into mine. Something about them sent a deadly chill down my spine. It was the first time I'd seen his eyes up close. I couldn't put my finger on why I had such a visceral reaction to his eyes. It didn't make sense. I brushed the fear away. I needed to be fierce.

I could feel his breath. Just a little bit closer. My forehead could feasibly break his nose, sending the shards up into his skull and killing him instantly. If I only aimed it right.

Arching my neck, I thrust my head forward with all my strength, prepared for the blow of striking him, but he drew back in time, leaving me hitting nothing but air until my chin touched my chest.

"But our subjects keep dying," he said, continuing to talk as if nothing had happened. "It's truly unfortunate. We're lucky that so many runaways are addicts. We have an endless supply."

"What's in the needle?"

"A new type of opiate. Somewhat like a liquid fentanyl."

"I don't understand. I thought you were working on a remedy."

"You are now officially our twelfth subject. But we have a slight problem."

I drew back into the bed as much as I could. "What's that?"

"You are not an addict."

Dragon Lady's head popped up behind King's shoulder. "Don't worry, honey. It won't take long and you will be very happy. Perhaps the happiest you've ever been. See, we're going after it from both ends. We're manufacturing an irresistible, highly-addictive opiate and also the only effective cure for the country's addiction epidemic at the same time. We'll profit enormously from the problem and the solution—and we'll be the only ones who have both."

Fear coursed through me, and no matter how hard I tried to hide it, I knew King could see it in my eyes. I'd spent a portion of the last year being drugged by a boyfriend who ended up being a serial killer. Drugs scared the shit out of me, now. Well, except weed, that is. Weed didn't scare me, but that didn't really count.

"This is a mistake, King." I tried to make my voice sound as badass as possible, but it was slightly shrill. King was scooping up runaways, using them like guinea pigs, and then discarding them when they died. And now I was caught up in his depraved ideology and his plans to hurt as many people as possible to get what he wanted.

"Yes, it's truly unfortunate," he said. "Every time we test out a new formula it fails. The last formulation, well, we thought it was ready, but that subject also died. You may have met her briefly. Layla."

Also died? How many girls had he killed? He said I was the twelfth subject. Fury surged through me. Just lean down a little more, fucker, so I can bash my head through your skull. This time I won't miss.

"You will be the first recipient of our new formula. It's almost ready. But first we must turn you into an addict. So, we are, as they say, dealing with apples to apples.

"I must confess that, as I mentioned, our success-to-failure rate is somewhat dismal, so I can't guarantee this new formula will work. My advice to you is to enjoy the last weeks of your life. White rapture will help with that."

Before I could react, King had found a plump vein and slipped the needle into my arm with a sneer. Warmth and a near-immediate sense of overwhelming well-being poured over me as the drug surged through my veins.

"Fuck you," I said. But the words came out sounding like "Fuggu."

Then I melted into the pillow with a disconcerting sense of wellness. It was all going to be just fine.

That night was full of strange dreams and nightmares. At one point a hand caressed my scar then trailed down my neck, my breast, my abdomen and then lingered between my legs. I gasped in pleasure. A voice whispered something in my ear and I found myself smiling.

Bobby.

My entire body was on fire. I stretched against something

holding me down, my mouth searching for another's mouth. But then the haze began to clear. I was in a room bound and drugged. King's prisoner.

I opened my eyes just as I heard the door click closed across the room.

23

I HATED MYSELF, BUT AS THE SWEAT DRIPPED FROM MY TEMPLES, I strained to hear footsteps in the hallway outside my room. All I wanted was for the Dragon Lady to walk in with that needle.

Anger bloomed in my core. It was *way* past time for my injection. I glanced at the clock on the wall. For the past few weeks, my world had revolved around that clock. Twice a day, when the hands on the clock rested on the eight and the twelve, I got a dose of the drug. Then, I'd spend the next twelve hours in a haze of contentment while I waited. Despite what King said, I still held out hope that my text to James had gotten through, and that he was going to find me any time. Might as well enjoy the relaxation. I wasn't sure how long I'd been prisoner. I'd started to keep track but then when the drugs hit my system, days blurred into nights in my windowless room and I began confused.

Despite my craving for the drugs blotting out everything else, there still was a black, floating cloud in my mind that I kept pushing back. Django. I refused to allow myself to think about my dog. Every time the cloud hovered nearby, I mentally drop kicked it away.

It was only during the moments when the exhilaration of the drug had faded and I was waiting for the next dose that the unease grew in me. Images of Django limp on my rooftop. Flashbacks of Bobby's bloody body in Positano. A quick flash of Layla, so tiny in that hospital bed, hooked up to the countless wires and tubes that had only prolonged the inevitable just long enough for her mother to rub her cold feet.

Along with the memory of Layla, was the certainty that other girls had died—and more still would—if I didn't do something.

It was then that I would chafe at the binds holding me down. Sweat would drip down my temples as I exhausted myself trying to get free. Then I would lie back and my mind would race with ways I might be able to escape. Each time, I came up empty. But I didn't give up. I knew there had to be a way. I had nothing to do for hours but brainstorm where the weaknesses were. What was the Dragon Lady's weakness? I had yet to see King again. She was the one I needed to beat first. There had to be something, some way to escape.

Nothing was impossible.

I had to believe that.

Today, though, something was different. Usually when I received my dose, I still had a slight comforting glow remaining from the last injection. But today, the drug had completely worn off, and I was experiencing withdrawal symptoms. I felt like I was going to vomit, and my stomach cramped painfully. It wasn't the worst pain I'd ever felt, but it still sucked.

At the same time, I was overcome with nearly crippling anxiety. A terrible feeling of dread suffused me. Withdrawal. Hadn't it only been a little more than a week? Could someone become addicted so quickly?

The sick feeling was tinged with fury. My rage was laced with a heavy dose of guilt and a bit of fear. I was probably going to die here. What a stupid way to go. They would try out the latest formula on me any day and I'd die from it. And the worst part of all was that I wouldn't be dying for anything worthwhile. And others would die because of my failure.

I knew that at least one other girl was being held here: Josie. I'd seen her.

Each day, Dragon Lady walked me down the hall to an industrial size bathroom and shower. Even though most of the time I was already high and had lost my focus on escaping a little, I used those walks as reconnaissance. Most of the time, the doors lining the hallway were closed. But every once in a while, they were cracked open. Curtains blocked my view of the interior of the rooms. But I heard girl's voices.

One day, I heard a familiar voice as we came upon an open door. "Hello? Who is that?" I shouted. My voice was weak and cracked. I'd barely spoken for most of my time here. But she screamed back. "Who are you?"

There were sounds of a scuffle. The curtain was thrown back just as we passed. A wan face appeared for a second before it was yanked back behind the curtain.

It was that girl Josie. Jesus. How had she ended back up in here? "Josie!" I screamed it. "It's Gia." I began to struggle. But the Dragon Lady pushed the tranquilizer gun into my back and forced me to move on.

"Josie!" I screamed again. "I'm going to get us out of here."

The girl burst into hysterical laughter punctuated by sobs before her door slammed shut and I couldn't hear anything anymore.

She would die along with the rest of us. Who was I to promise to help her?

If I knew I was going to die saving the lives of all the other girls King was experimenting on, then at least I could die in peace.

But as it was, I was going to die for nothing. My only consolation was that in death I might see Bobby again. And my parents. I wasn't sure how I felt about the afterlife, but I did think there was a chance. My mother's Catholic faith was so strong when I was growing up that I couldn't help but think maybe there was something to her unwavering belief that we never truly die. She was the most intelligent person I knew, and when I openly doubted her belief once, she sat me down and explained how energy never dies.

The memory of my mother was like a punch in the gut. I didn't want to think about her right then. The shame of imagining that she could somehow see me now. My weakness. My ease in succumbing to the drug.

I struggled against the restraints on my wrists, grimacing and straining until my face felt hot. The door swung open and tears of relief slipped from my eyes and down my cheeks onto the coarse pillow beneath my head that was beginning to smell foul.

Instead of instantly tying up my upper arm and injecting me, the Dragon Lady stood over me and smiled. I was confused until she took one long manicured fingernail and wiped a stray tear. She put her fingertip to her mouth and smiled even more.

"Please?" I was pleading. I stared at the needle in her other hand. I hated the sound of my voice. "Please?"

She pressed her lips together and looped the rubber tourniquet around my arm. But instead of injecting me, she held the needle aloft and leaned over me. With her other hand, she took one long, pointed fingernail and gingerly traced the scar that ran from my temple to my cheekbone.

"He marked you. Do not forget this. Even in death, you are his. As I am."

Drawing away from me, she pulled down the collar of her

shirt. I recoiled, but saw a thick, pink scar that ran from the base of her neck to her collarbone.

Then she stuck me with the sharp tip of the needle, turning my objections into pure bliss. As I faded into a soft memory of my mother, I heard the Dragon Lady speaking to someone.

I pushed reality away and submerged myself in the memory of my mother and the smile on her face Christmas morning as she watched me open my biggest present—a Barbie sports car. I jumped up and down with excitement. I hadn't wanted a Barbie house or horse or clothes. I'd wanted something to race around the house like my brother Christopher did with his cars. The faster the better. And I was overjoyed—it wasn't the pink Ferrari convertible. It was the red one! Just like I'd asked Santa for.

But in the back of my mind, something was nagging at me. I knew I should be alarmed. It was something that didn't fit into my dreaming about my Barbie car. a voice saying, "She is ready."

24

LATER THAT DAY, THE DRAGON LADY ROLLED AN IV POLE INTO MY room. A bag with blue liquid hung from it. It didn't look like the normal sugar water or whatever it was they gave me instead of food.

I didn't say a word.

"This is step one. Tomorrow you get the antidote to White Rapture. We must prep you."

"Fuck you." I said it with a smile. I was feeling good. Better than that, even. I didn't want to admit it, but whatever they gave me made me feel fucking fantastic. Better than the best sex. Better than the most pristine and expensive bottle of bourbon. Better than racing my Ferrari down the coastal roads of Big Sur.

Nothing—*nothing*—compared to how I felt with this drug inside me.

It was terrifying. And brilliant.

She ignored me. "This may make you vomit. Try not to choke on it. That is not a good way to go."

"Like you care."

She uncapped my open IV line and I watched detachedly as

the blue liquid trickled down the clear tube and entered my arm.

"Do you feel sick?"

I didn't feel anything so I shook my head.

"Sometimes it hits later. Or maybe you're just lucky," she said, her voice echoing oddly as she walked out of my sightline and toward the door.

I gave a strangled laugh and said, "I'm never lucky."

I fell asleep tossing and turning, sweating and fearful.

Sometime in the night, I awoke, adrenaline zipping through me.

I still felt the warm haze of the opiate in my system, but my mind was suddenly clear and sharp. I'd been looking for a chink in their armor, and it had come to me in the black of night.

I had a plan.

Once a day, they took me to the bathroom down the hall. Instead of my regular restraints, they zip tied my wrists. Since they couldn't keep my ankles bound and expect me to walk, Dragon Lady also held a dart gun to my back as we made our way down the hallway to the bathroom. I'd carefully memorized every door we passed on our way, including the one where Josie was, and I knew at the end of the hall was a door leading outside since light filtered through its small window.

When I used the toilet, the Dragon Lady kept the bathroom door open, watching me. I'd quickly got used to it and was no longer embarrassed to have her watch my lame efforts to wipe myself with my wrists bound in front of me.

Whatever sustenance they gave me through the IV fortunately stifled my bowel movements. But the one time I'd had one, the Dragon Lady had blanched and grimaced and looked away.

"Why don't you at least untie me, so I can properly wipe?"

I watched her profile. She wouldn't turn her head to look at me. And it looked like she was holding her breath.

But she did. She cut off the zip ties and held the tranquilizer gun pointed at my chest, saying if it hit my heart I'd probably die.

In her eyes, my only shot at escaping was during the moment she took of my zip ties. The rest of the time, her guard was down. It was a weakness I was going to exploit the hell out of.

Kato had once taught me how to escape if my wrists were tied with duct tape that involved a focused thrust of my arms back toward the sides of my ribcage that was powerful enough to rip the tape. I had no idea if it would work on zip ties, but it was all I had. I'd run out of time.

Now, it was time to put on an act worthy of an Oscar. My best bet was to escape in the dead of night while any other clinic staff would be gone.

The Dragon Lady had said that the blue liquid made some people sick.

I decided to be "some people" and to take advantage of her obvious revulsion to, well, shit.

"Hey!" My voice was hoarse. I didn't recognize the sound that came out. My vocal cords hadn't been used more than a handful of times in the entire time I'd been here. I cleared my throat and tried again. "Hey!"

Nothing.

Then I got into it. I screamed. A real scream. As if a monster had just popped up from under my bed. Or the gurney. Or whatever the fuck this thing was.

I screamed again and again. I heard muffled voices in the hall. I remained silent for a second and then shouted. "Help. Please. I feel like I'm going to puke."

I didn't hear anything so I upped the ante. I was fairly certain the Dragon Lady would do anything to avoid having to deal with me shitting my bed.

"I need to use the bathroom. Number two. Actually, number two mixed with number one. I can't hold it in. I need to go to the bathroom. I can't hold it anymore. If you don't come there's going to be a huge mess."

That did it. The door swung open, and the overhead lights blared on, blinding me for a second. When I could see again, I saw Dragon Lady before me. I grimaced.

"I really need to go."

She nodded at some lackey, a dude I only saw when it was time to make my daily bathroom trip. He had messy hair and thick glasses and a puffy face. He always wore scrubs and was about six inches shorter than me, but I knew he had muscles. I'd felt them when he hoisted me off and back onto the gurney each day. He undid my straps while Dragon Lady held the tranq gun on me until the zip ties bound my wrists. For the past God-knows-how-many-times they'd done this, I'd used an FBI tactic to make sure the ties were put on loosely.

It involved holding my elbows tightly at my ribcage and making my hands wide open as opposed to fists. By doing this, it expanded my forearms as large as they would go. I stayed tensed like this until the zip ties were on and the scrubs guy stepped away.

"Go," she said yawning. I noted her silky robe thrown over what looked like black pajama pants and soft slippers.

Perfect. She'd been asleep.

"Go," she said again, and gestured with the gun toward the door. I knew the routine. As soon as we stepped into the hall, the door to my room slammed behind us. The scrubs guy waited inside the room to help me back on the gurney when I returned. I'd never understood why he hadn't come along too in case I tried to escape, but now I'd use that to my advantage.

I assumed it had to do with the Dragon Lady's arrogance and misplaced confidence in her abilities to match me physically. She was mistaken in thinking the tranquilizer gun was all she needed to keep me under control.

Now, with the door closed behind us, I whirled to face her. She had yet to bring the gun up and was in the middle of another yawn. I bashed my head into her forehead, sending her plunging to the ground with a yelp. At the same time, I swung toward my door and engaged the deadbolt lock using my bound hands, trapping the orderly inside. I heard murmured shouting and pounding on the other side of the door.

The Dragon Lady surprised me with a scissor kick from the ground that almost sent me sprawling. I regained my footing and dropped. I pinned her to the floor with my knees on her elbows and my fingers at her throat in a choke hold. Her eyes bulged.

I didn't want to kill her. I only wanted to make her pass out. I was about to let off the pressure when she slammed her knees into my back, knocking the wind out of me. I rolled off her, reeling and gasping for air. She was up and on me before I could breathe again. This time she held a hypodermic needle. I managed to keep the gleaming needle in her hand at arm's length, but my grip was slipping. I was weak. I'd been tied to a bed for days and hadn't had real food in just as long. The needle grew closer to my face. Jesus! I realized she was trying to stab me in the eye.

I released the pressure on her wrist and directed her blow to the side of my head where the needle struck the ground and clattered out of her grasp. At the same time, I smashed my elbow into her jaw. Before I could roll to the side, she landed a punch to my temple. But I'd taken worse blows.

We wrestled and I came out ahead, once again holding her down. This time I reached over and grabbed the needle, plunging it into her neck. I watched her eyes loll back until I only saw white. I scooped up the tranquilizer gun. There was no place to stick it when wearing a hospital gown.

Meanwhile, the scrubs guy was still on the other side of the door, pounding away like a lunatic. I didn't know who else stayed here overnight, but I couldn't count on these two being the only ones staffing the building. I raced for the door at the end of the hall. Halfway there the lights went out and an alarm sounded. The hall was lit with a red light that allowed me to see, but flickered eerily. I'd just about reached the door when I heard a sickening sound—the clank of a heavy metal door slamming into place.

A speaker crackled to life. King's voice sent terror streaking through me. "There is nowhere to run, Gia."

25

KING.

A surveillance camera swiveled as I walked underneath it. I jumped but couldn't reach it. I didn't have time to try to disable it.

I whirled and raced back to the Dragon Lady. Yanking at her kimono, I searched for pockets. I found a small pocket with a keycard in it.

Back at the exit door, I pressed the card to the keypad, but the light on it remained red.

At the opposite end of the hall I saw another small red light. Another keypad. I ran, jumping over the Dragon Lady's body. She was moaning, but not moving. The scrubs guy kept screaming from behind my locked door.

This time when I pressed the key card to the pad, the light flashed green, and I yanked on the handle. The door opened into some type of living quarters. I took it all in as snapshots as I ran through looking for an exit. The space contained a great room with a combo kitchen area and living room and then a hallway led to a series of bedrooms and bathrooms. It was only when I got to the master bedroom—appointed in dark heavy furniture—that I saw my only chance.

French doors led to a balcony.

I raced onto the balcony and peered over the edge. Some hedges would cushion my fall. We were only on the third story. I had one leg over the rail when it hit me.

Josie. *Shit.*

Back in the bedroom, I ripped the drawers out of the dresser searching for a weapon. Anything more powerful than this tranquilizer gun. I pulled on some black leggings and a black T-shirt I found in the drawer, ditching my hospital gown and tucking my gun into the tight, elastic waistband. I paused, listening for any sound outside the door.

Hearing nothing, I raced to a closet to search for shoes.

The interior was like the dressing area of a fancy boutique. A chaise lounge. Several end tables. Mirrors.

Several shelves of designer stilettos greeted me.

I got on my hands and knees on the closet floor and found some Givenchy running shoes. I examined them and immediately tossed them across the room. They were about three sizes too small. Bare feet then.

A sound outside the large walk in closet made me freeze. I reached for a marble statue sitting on an end table and ducked back into a row of long dresses where I crouched on the floor, clutching the figurine of some Greek goddess in one hand and the tranquilizer gun in the other. Just as the dresses settled back into place, I heard heavy breathing and saw some black shoes step into the carpeted closet.

I wanted to take out the person's shins and knees with the statue, but when I arched my arm back I banged into the wall. The shoes stopped moving and I knew I was made. Right when he parted the dresses to look for me I smashed the statue into his face. He reeled back at the same time I kicked him in the chest, sending him whirling into the opposite wall of clothes. I stepped out of the dresses and now, with room to swing, landed another blow with the statue.

That one dropped him to the floor. I barely took him in. Some bulky thug I'd never seen before. I dropped the statue and searched him. He had a small silver gun. I grabbed it and stepped out of the closet.

My breath caught at what I saw.

King stood with his back to me, facing the French doors. He wore a dark suit even though I'd obviously disturbed him from sleep. His hands were interlaced behind his back.

"You can shoot me right now if you want," he said. "But I know you won't."

My arms shook, the gun wavering wildly.

He continued. "Renaldo was the only bodyguard I have on premises. It will be a few minutes before anyone else arrives."

"What's your game, King?"

"There is no game."

"Bullshit."

I lowered the gun. He was right. I couldn't shoot him in the back.

Inching toward the door, I kept my eye on him.

"Why are you going to let me go?"

"You can't escape your destiny. You are mine."

"Bullshit," I said again.

He turned. "You've taken out my men. You have a gun. I don't."

"That didn't stop you before."

He cocked his head and I could almost feel a burning sensation as his eyes searched my scar.

"It's sexy. You were too, let's say, *perfect*, to be beautiful before."

"Fuck you."

He took a step forward. I raised the gun again.

He laughed.

That's when I noticed an old-fashioned landline phone. It was on the dresser near me.

"Get in the closet," I ordered.

As I said it, I heard a car's tires squealing. And then another. The troops had arrived. I reached over, plucked the phone off the receiver. Punched in 911.

"Help. He's got a gun. Kraig King. And I think he killed someone."

King remained expressionless. I hung up and backed toward the door.

Once in the hallway, I slammed the door behind me and raced to the room where I'd seen Josie before. I was expecting to hear King's footsteps behind me, but the hall remained quiet. Swiping the keypad, I sighed in relief when I heard a click.

The door flew open before I could grab the handle. Josie. She stood there in her hospital gown, scowling. I quickly guided her back to the living area and the bedroom beyond. I entered holding the gun in front of me. I whirled, sweeping the gun in an erratic arc to clear the space. King was gone.

"The balcony," I said to Josie.

We were both over the edge, had landed on the dirt below, and were racing away when I heard sirens in the distance.

The clinic was up a windy road, and by cutting through the brush, we created a shortcut to the main highway down below. We slid down a grassy hill, crossed the road, and slid down another hill before I dared to try to flag down a ride.

The first driver veered wildly to the opposite lane to avoid us even getting close. I'm sure we looked like the walking dead. The second one did the same. I backed off onto the shoulder, but nobody would stop.

I grew desperate as my weariness caught up to me. Josie stood slightly behind me, breathing heavily. I was worried about her.

As a cone of headlights neared, I stepped into the middle of the road and held my breath. The driver of the oncoming SUV slammed on her brakes.

"Are you insane!" The woman had rolled down her window and yelled at me, but I was faster than her.

I was in her passenger seat before she could roll her window back up and lock her doors. Josie popped open the back door and jumped inside.

The driver screamed. She tried to unlock her door to get out, but I hit the locks on my side.

"Hey, I'm harmless, but the guys after me aren't. Let's get out of here."

Her eyes darted toward her dash. Her phone was sticking to it, showing some map. I ripped it off the Velcro and kept it in my palm by the door.

"You don't have to take us far. Just get us away from here, okay?"

I looked in the rearview mirror. I saw a black SUV approaching. It could be King. Or not. But I couldn't take a chance. I slumped in the seat. I saw Josie do the same. "*Drive!* They'll happily kill you just to get to us."

Our driver began to hyperventilate. But she finally put one leather beige pump on the gas, and we took off.

"Step on it," I said. "The speed limit's sixty-five here, right?"

The car accelerated. I stayed crouched.

"Is there still a big black SUV behind us?"

I watched her profile. Sweat dripped down her temples and her pulse throbbed in her neck. She glanced in the rear-view mirror. "I don't see...Oh, yes."

"How far back?"

"Two, maybe three cars?"

"Okay. I'm going to crawl in the back now. Don't try anything funny, okay?"

She nodded.

I crawled into the back with Josie and lay on the floorboards. It was only then that I realized I was sweaty and weak and dizzy. My body ached from my fight with the Dragon Lady. The adrenaline had kept me going, but now I wanted to lie down and give up. But we still weren't safe. I glanced around.

Josie was curled so tightly into a ball on the seat that anyone looking in wouldn't know it was a person there. I tried to squish against the door to become as small as I could so nobody could see me, either.

"Now, I want you to slow down—not so much that it's suspicious—but slow enough so that the other cars start to pass you. Are you in the slow or fast lane?"

"Fast."

"Take your foot off the gas very slightly. Whatever you do, don't use the brakes. Now slow down slightly and get in the far-right lane, so that other cars pass you."

She didn't argue. She put her signal on and I felt the car swerve to the right. A little too rapidly, but it was okay.

"Where's the SUV now?"

"Right behind us."

Shit. "In this lane? In the same lane?"

"Yes. Wait, it's going to pass."

"Okay. Don't look over whatever you do."

She started crying. "What if they have a gun? You said they wanted to kill you?"

"As long as you keep your cool, you'll be fine."

A loud sob escaped her. "Oh my God. I don't want to die."

"Shut up," I said.

It was harsh, but it worked. After all, I was trying to save our lives. She immediately stopped crying.

A few seconds later she burst into tears again.

I was about to roll my eyes when she said, "They went right by. They're way ahead of us now."

"Now look in your rearview mirror."

"Okay." She was calm now.

"Are there any other cars behind you?"

"No."

"Are you sure?" I sat up anyway before she answered.

The black SUV was a dark spot on the horizon. There were no cars behind us. I patted her shoulder. She jumped, nearly smacking her head on the ceiling of the car.

"You did great."

"Fuck you."

I laughed. "After we make sure the SUV passes it, take the next exit."

We sat in the parking lot of a gas station while I called James with our reluctant get-away driver's phone. The sun was rising to the west behind us. It went straight to voice mail. I left a brief message.

"James, I was kidnapped. I was held prisoner at this address." I reeled off the address of the rehab facility. You have to go rescue anyone else who is there, and shut it down. Tell your sergeant. Bring a SWAT team. They're experimenting on young girls and the girls are dying. I managed to get one girl out, but I'm certain they have more."

The driver shot me a startled glance, and I opened my eyes wide and nodded at her. *See? I wasn't fucking around, lady.*

After I hung up, I dialed Tony. I glanced at Josie. Our next stop would have to be the hospital. She didn't look good.

"You can leave as soon as our car arrives," I told the woman. "If you give me your address, I can send you cash to reimburse your account."

She glared at me.

"Or not?" I said.

26

A NURSE RACED OUT OF THE ER DOORS, FOLLOWED BY SEVERAL orderlies, one of whom pushed a gurney in front of him. It helped that Tony had screeched into the parking lot and laid on the horn.

I was lucky he'd been close by when I called.

I opened my door and threw Josie's arms around my shoulders. She was like a limp doll. The ER workers took her from me and put her on the gurney.

"She needs help. She's addicted to opiates and in withdrawals. Her pulse is weak."

I could as easily have been speaking about myself.

As if he'd read my mind, the nurse gave me the once over. "You look like you might need to be checked out yourself."

"No." I leaned over the girl. Her eyes were wide and terrified. "You'll be okay. I'll check on you later."

She swallowed and nodded.

I forced a smile. "You're going to be fine."

Turning toward the nurse who seemed in charge, I met his eyes. "Don't let anybody in to see her. Not even her family. In fact, call the police. She's been held captive and drugged for weeks. She's going to need a guard outside her room to keep them from getting to her."

It might have sounded cruel to keep her family away, but right then, I didn't trust King's men not to say they were relatives. Her own family could wait until James could make sure an armed officer was posted outside her door.

I was hesitant to leave her, but I needed to get the hell out of there.

The nurse grabbed my arm, and I yanked it away. "Don't fucking touch me."

Back in the car, I asked Tony for his phone and called James again. Straight to voice mail. He might not be picking up because of the unfamiliar phone numbers. I mean, cops had to be careful about stuff like that, right?

"James. Gia again. I just dropped a girl named Josie off at United General. I think she'll need an armed officer or guard. I don't think King wants her talking. She's a liability." I paused. "I hope you get this."

I hung up and handed Tony his phone.

"Where to next?" he said. His eyes raked over my face. "You don't look so hot."

"So, I've been told. That nurse might have written down your license plate."

"What? Who cares? I'm not allowed to drive a customer?"

"You're right. You're good. Let's go."

I gave him my home address again. Five minutes later, his phone dinged. He glanced down and then handed it to me.

"Copy. J."

Short and terse, but at least I knew he'd received my message. Thank God. I slumped in the seat. I wasn't sure I'd even have the energy to push the elevator button to my loft and crawl into my bed.

27

I LET MYSELF INTO MY LOFT WITH TREPIDATION. DJANGO.

During my captivity, I'd held on to one small sliver of hope: that Thanh-Thanh had noticed I was missing and had hunted down Django's vet. And most of all—that my dog was still alive.

If he was dead. I'd want to die. For sure.

I left bloody footprints behind me as I walked up the stairs to my place. The pads of my feet were shredded from tromping through the brush and down the hills as we escaped. I didn't realize until too late that I didn't have the elevator key that would take me from the garage directly to the inside of my loft. I'd have to rectify that and put a digital keypad on the elevator like I had on the door to my loft.

On my way up, I stopped at every floor, trying not to throw up. When I'd start again, I pulled myself along with help from the rails. Sweat poured down my face. I didn't think I'd make it. My legs felt weak. And I was so nauseous. Opioid withdrawals at its finest. If I could only make it to my bed. It would take a few days, but I'd suffer through the withdrawal symptoms on my own, behind my reinforced steel door.

When I finally made it to the top floor and my door, my

hands and fingers were shaking so badly that it took me a few tries to punch in the right code on the keypad. I swung open my door afraid to even breathe. My lights were on. I held the thug's little silver gun out in front of me and peeked inside. No Django came running to greet me.

I glanced over at the alcove where I kept Django's bowls for food and water. One bowl had water in it. The other was empty. I had no idea if this was good or bad.

And my place? From what I could see in the doorway, it was spotless. Something was up.

I usually had clothes everywhere and sometimes—okay, a lot of the times—dirty dishes in the sink. Somebody must have been here. Which meant Django was fine, right? Anxiety overcame me. I felt a ball of panic soar from my stomach into my throat, and it was suddenly hard to get air into my lungs.

Confident no one was hiding in the shadows to kill me, I stepped inside and saw that the door to the roof was open. Thank God. Django might be on the roof. But usually if he's up there, when I get home, he races down with the joyous racket of a herd of buffalo. My heart was now pounding all the way up in my throat. I was about to give my little special whistle for him when I heard footsteps on the ceiling above. Someone was on the roof.

I crept toward the door to the stairs and heard whining. Relief flooded me. Then I saw him. My beloved dog. A hunched shadow at the top of the stairs whining. I started to smile and call him when the words died in my throat. Why wouldn't he come down?

I raised the gun and, with my back against one wall of the stairway, slowly made my way up. Django stood and wagged his tail so hard it thumped against the walls. When I got nearly to the top of the stairs I stretched, reaching over to pat him under the jaw, keeping my eyes beyond him, waiting to see who was on the roof. I didn't see anything. I took another step and scratched him behind the ears, keeping my eyes trained on the doorway behind him. I was ready to loop my fingers through his collar and yank him down the stairs if I sensed any danger.

I didn't like that he was the only thing between me and whomever was walking on my roof. A person who apparently didn't feel it necessary to call out to me.

I took another step.

My head popped up, and I could see above and past my dog.

That's when I saw her.

My mouth opened in surprise. Like an idiot, I stood there speechless.

There, under the grape arbor, stretched out in my lounge chair was my aunt.

The Queen of Spades.

28

I STEPPED ONTO THE ROOF AND STOOD THERE WITH MY ARMS folded across my chest.

She finished a sip of something in a coffee mug, smiled at me, and then stood.

"I could've used your help earlier today," I said. "Or actually for the past few weeks."

She walked toward me. For a second the sun was behind her and she looked like a specter. I'd forgotten how tall she was. Freakishly tall. Like Amazonian. Over six feet, I bet. But then I saw that while she was tall, she also wore thigh-high black boots with four-inch heels. With serious tread on them. I took in the rest of her: Above the boots were leather leggings and a black long-sleeve T-shirt. She looked just like she did when I met her in Sicily.

She walked over. As she did, I searched her face. It's so strange to look at her. Her features are so much like mine. But she had faint smile lines around her eyes and mouth. And her cheekbones were more drawn.

She leaned over and kissed each one of my cheeks European style.

"You look ill." She said it matter-of-fact. Like she wasn't surprised. Or even concerned.

Django—the traitor—sat at her feet and looked adoringly up at her. You'd have thought he'd be slobbering all over me after not seeing me for weeks.

"I've been drugged. I think I'm in withdrawal."

She nodded. "I think you're right."

"Why? What?" I gestured in a circle, at a loss for words.

"I just got to town," she said with an accent. Her cool gaze continued to take me in. "I left as soon as I received word that you were missing."

I narrowed my eyes. "Left where? Where do you live? Who told you anyway?"

She didn't answer, just walked past me and down the stairs. Django gave me a guilty look, and with his tail down, trailed after her.

I sunk into one of the patio chairs under the grape arbor. I felt a wave of nausea. Maybe I should have a drink. Or a smoke. Something. Get some type of drug into my body since I wouldn't be getting any more opioids.

I leaned over a potted plant near my chaise lounge, but my fingers hit dirt. My pack of cigarettes was gone. I went over to a small bench with a lid and opened it. I had a case of smokes stashed there. Gone.

The movement made me retch. I turned, wide-eyed, and looked over at my bar. The glasses were still there, but the booze was gone. All of it.

What the—?

Then I was dry heaving. Holding onto the rail for dear life, I made my way down the stairs and nearly collapsed at the bottom, sitting down hard on the last step. I leaned over and dry heaved again.

"Let's get you to bed." She took my arm and lifted me to

standing. She was surprisingly strong. Then she looped another arm around my waist and practically carried me to my bed. I crawled under the covers and wanted to cry with relief but instead had to sit up and lean over the side of the bed to dry-heave again.

My aunt crossed the loft to my galley kitchen. She cracked open the refrigerator, leaned over and peered inside, and began pulling items out to the counter.

I tilted my head. The fridge was full. Of *green stuff*. Produce, it appeared.

As my aunt slapped a bunch of green things I didn't recognize onto my counter, she softly hummed a song that was hauntingly familiar.

"What is that? That song?" I said and tried to sit up. I searched my memory. I knew it somehow. But the only image that came to mind was my mother's smiling face.

"It's a song my mother—your grandmother—used to sing to us as children."

"Oh my God." My mother had sung it to me in my crib. The image flashed so vividly in my mind that it brought tears to my eyes. I'd never had a memory go back that far.

I tried to hide my tears, but my aunt was now busy putting food in Django's dish.

"Who was taking care of Django this whole time?" I said to change the subject.

"Your neighbor."

Thanh-Thanh. Like I thought.

I eyed the stuff on the counter again. Looked like greens, a carton of blueberries, strawberries, and some jars of weird seeds.

"I thought you just got here."

She shrugged. "Yesterday."

Reaching across my counter, she plugged in a blender-type thing I'd never seen before.

Then she filled its glass pitcher with selections from all the food on the counter.

"What's that?"

"Your dinner."

I laughed. "I've been eating out of an IV for God knows how long. The last thing I want is a liquid meal. As soon as I don't want to vomit anymore, I'm ordering a steak and potatoes and red wine...and...where are my cigarettes and alcohol?" I glanced at the counter where I usually kept a big bottle of bourbon. In its place was a weird jar with some floating placenta or something inside. A scrap of paper had feminine writing on it that said, "Kombucha."

I turned toward her. "For instance, where is my Old Fitzgerald Whiskey I was saving for a special occasion. The one that cost three thousand dollars?"

She shrugged. "I threw them all away."

I eyed the trash chute. Maybe a few bottles were still intact in the basement trash area. After all, they could have landed on something soft, like another trash bag.

"You're sick. And as soon as you get better we begin training."

She pressed a button and the buzzing of the blender drowned out my words of confusion. Training?

When the contents of the glass jar had turned into a brownish green liquid, she stopped the blender and poured the mush into a big glass. She walked over to me and put it into my hand. I caught a whiff of a familiar scent.

That's when I remembered she wore the same perfume as my mother.

"We begin full-on training as soon as you feel better. Maybe in three days," she said, sitting at the café table and watching me. "I think you should have a few days to rest and recover from your ordeal."

"What day *is* it?"

"It's October twenty-third."

I'd been held prisoner for twenty days.

"Drink that please," she said.

"Thanks for your generosity." I scrunched my face. "But I really need a drink drink. Not this. Alcohol."

"You actually don't," she said. She sat so still it made me uncomfortable. "This is the perfect time to quit drinking. You haven't had a drink in weeks. Or a cigarette."

"Which is why I want one," I said and put the glass of gunk down on my nightstand.

"It actually tastes better than it looks. It has ginger in it as well. That will calm your stomach."

I made a face.

"What's all this about training?" I said.

But she was back poking around inside my cupboards. Even from my bed I could see that most of my crap food was gone—cookies, crackers, peanut butter-filled pretzels. Instead, they'd been replaced with cans of beans and tuna and. to my surprise, boxes of pasta, although it was a brand I didn't recognize.

"Pasta made the cut, huh?" I said.

"I *am* Sicilian," she said.

A phone rang and I jumped. It was my aunt's cell phone. She took it up to the roof with Django trailing at her heels. I ignored the glass of mush beside me and lay back down. I fell asleep before she returned.

29

I spent three days in bed, lifting my head occasionally to vomit as I got over the withdrawal symptoms.

My aunt made me sit up and drink some weird bitter tasting concoction every hour, which probably kept me from ending up in the hospital from dehydration.

I knew her name was Eva, but I couldn't think of her as anything other than "my aunt," or "the Queen of Spades." It somehow seemed too personal to consider calling her Aunt Eva. I mean she was a blood relative, but where had she been all my life? She looked like an older version of me, smelled like my mother's perfume, and hummed songs that reminded me of my childhood, and yet she was essentially a stranger.

And she was here in my sacred space—my loft, my home—nursing me while I purged all the drugs out of my body.

In the distant haze of my mind I wanted to watch the news to see if they had busted the rehab facility, but all I could concentrate on was trying not to lift my head because it made me barf.

That night, I felt normal enough to call Darling with a burner phone the Queen had left by my bed in case of an emergency while she was out and about. I had no idea what she was up to but she'd leave for an hour at a time and then return without any explanation.

Darling gasped when she heard my voice, and it filled me with shame for not calling her immediately. I filled her in on everything that had happened.

"I reported you missing." She sounded stuffed up. Was she crying?

"You did? Didn't James let you know I texted him the other day?"

"No, he didn't." She sounded angry at first, but then her voice softened. "But I can tell you that he was worried sick."

"Could've fooled me. He hasn't been by here."

"Hmmm," Darling said. "There's something going on. He said he couldn't talk to me about it, but to tell you he'd be in touch."

"Because it was too hard to come here and tell me himself?" My voice oozed bitterness.

"Gia." Her voice was slightly scolding.

"I got one of the girls out. You remember Josie?"

As I said it, panic streamed through me. I hadn't been in touch. I hadn't called the hospital to see if she was okay.

"Josie showed up at her house the other day," Darling said. "The police dropped her off. She wouldn't talk about where she was. Said she's afraid the white-haired man would come back and get her if she said anything. I didn't know you were there with her. That you were the one who helped her escape."

"My God, that poor girl."

But hearing Darling's account of Josie's reunion with her family sent an alarm through me. If Josie had spoken to the police, why was she still afraid? Something wasn't right. And what about the other two girls?

"Gia, I want to come see you with my own two eyes. Make

sure you're really okay, but me and George are on our way to the airport to go visit his mama in Philadelphia."

"Tell George hey for me."

I heard him answer. "Gia, thank God you are safe, woman."

When Darling got back on the line, I said, "Don't you worry about me. My aunt is here taking care of me."

"What aunt? The knife-fighting Sicilian one?"

"That's the one."

"Okay, then I won't worry about you while I'm gone."

"Good plan."

After we hung up, I dialed James again. Straight to voice mail.

My heart sunk. He knew I was home, and he couldn't even bother to come check on me.

My aunt woke me at 5:00 a.m. the next morning.

"Time to begin training."

She was not smiling.

"What?" I sat up, bleary-eyed and blinking, trying to focus on the woman in front of me.

She wore black leggings, a gray hoodie, and ball cap that said "Bella." She held onto Django's leash.

"Right now?"

"*Sì, naturalmente.*"

I groaned but got up.

Ten minutes later we were at Golden Gate Park running with all the other crazy fuckers up this early. I hated to admit it, but it felt wonderful to feel normal again. The fresh air on my face was rejuvenating. I was alive. And didn't want to barf for the first time in days.

My aunt held Django's leash and made easy conversation with me as I panted, my laboring breaths sending puffs of steam into the cold morning air.

"After we run, we begin your Gladiatura Moderna training. Four hours a day. Every day."

Part of me was thrilled. I'd been slightly obsessed with the ancient Sicilian martial arts form that concentrated on using swords and daggers and sticks since I'd come across my aunt's army of female assassins training in this manner.

I'd been training on my own but hadn't really found anyone who knew the ancient art well enough to help me accelerate my learning.

"I know a little."

"I know," she said. Of course, she did. She fucking knew everything. It was creepy. "But you need my help to achieve expertise."

I didn't argue.

"San Francisco is quite cold for September," she said, apparently changing the subject. Unlike me, she wasn't out of breath. In fact, she sounded like she was stretched out on a chaise lounge getting a massage, not huffing and puffing as we completed our second mile.

"It gets warmer in about a month," I said, panting. "Hey, can we take a break? I'm really out of shape."

"When you think you can't go anymore? That's when you have actually only expended 40 percent of your ability."

"That's bullshit," I mumbled.

She laughed. "Oh, I bet my sister had fun with you as a teenager."

My face grew red. It was enough to make her slow down and stop. I stood with my hands on my knees trying to catch my breath.

"My sister adored you. You were the light of her life." Her voice was soft.

I scoffed. "Christopher was."

My aunt shook her head. "No. He needed her more than you

did, but she loved you more. You were so much like her. Not physically. But your personality."

"How do you know?"

"She wrote me."

I stopped breathing. "Do you have the letters?" I couldn't hide the eagerness in my voice.

Something ran across her face that I couldn't name, but it felt like the hand of death.

Her voice was dull. "They were destroyed in a fire."

Like my parents. Who were shot dead and then burned up when their assassin set their Swiss house on fire in an attempt to hide the evidence from the authorities.

"A fire?" I asked, wanting to know more.

For a second her eyes blazed at me and I drew back, my entire body suffused with fear.

"Let's go," she said. Her face shut down. It was as if a steel wall had been erected between us. I felt colder than I had all morning.

Fine. Two could play that game.

"I appreciate you bringing me back up to speed and helping me regain my strength, but I've got to go after King. I can't wait."

"A friend of yours called," she said.

For a second my heart stopped. James.

But she was talking about Danny.

"He's doing surveillance on the house where the drone came from. He will call us immediately if there is any movement. I searched the building the day I arrived. It's empty. If anyone comes or goes, we will know."

How much did she know?

"His drone can't be there twenty-four hours a day." I said. I was angry. *Stay out of my business, lady.*

"No, but there is a man who doesn't have a home who lives on the sidewalk outside the building. He was happy to help us."

"Oh, yeah, right." That guy I'd seen. "How much you paying him? I sure hope it's more than the supply of Oxy that King's paying him to keep his mouth shut. So, how much?"

"Nothing."

I narrowed my own eyes and looked at her with suspicion.

My aunt shrugged. "I helped him once, and he is very grateful."

"Once? When? Have you been here before?" I remembered finding her business card on my rooftop terrace after I'd returned from Italy. "Of course, you have. But how many times?"

"My job has taken me here a few times in the past."

"What is your job anyway?"

"It's complicated."

"We've got time."

"Not really. We have an appointment at your Dojo with Kato in fifteen minutes. The car is waiting at home. Let's go."

"Did anyone else call?"

"No."

On the drive to Chinatown, I thought about what she had said. She and Tony were chatting like old friends.

From what she'd told me she'd been in contact with Danny and even searched the building I'd suspected was King's head-quarters.

It made me wonder.

"Have you always kept tabs on me?" I asked, interrupting her conversation with Tony.

She stared out the window at the fog rolling in from the ocean. It took her a few seconds, but I saw her head nod slightly.

"Starting when?"

She turned to me. "When your mother died."

"Oh."

I had so many questions. Why had she stayed hidden for so

much of my life. And why hadn't she come to me when my parents were murdered. Nothing made sense.

"Why didn't I ever see you? Or meet you before Sicily?"

"You needed to make your own way."

"I was almost murdered several times. Is that what you mean?" My voice was sharp. Tony's eyes met mine in the rearview mirror.

My aunt closed her lips tightly. Conversation over.

Later, after we'd trained at the Dojo, I called James while she was in the shower. It went straight to voicemail again.

There was too much to say to just leave in a voice mail: The reason I didn't call you for so long is because I was kidnapped, remember? And why is Josie still afraid? Didn't you guys shut down King's place? What about those other girls? And now my vigilante aunt is here from Sicily. She helped me through opioid withdrawals, and now she is putting me through some type of crazy Italian boot camp.

I hung up the phone without speaking. But when my aunt got out of the shower, I told her I was worried that girls were still dying at the rehab place.

"It's gone."

"What?"

"I searched. There were no girls. I burned it down."

"You're fucking kidding me?"

She shook her head. Then she leaned over to towel dry her hair.

"Was there anything inside?"

She shook her head again.

"He took the girls somewhere else then," I said. "We have to find them."

"I know. I've been trying. But there is something concerning in the back of the facility. Maybe fresh graves. I haven't had time to investigate."

My mouth grew dry.

That night, after we'd gone for another run and spent three hours in Gladiatura Moderna training, we took plates of pasta with garlic and olive oil and a bottle of red wine up to the roof.

I was surprised that she downed her wine so quickly and poured another glass.

"You ask me why I never contact you."

Her English faltered a little with the second glass of wine, I noticed.

I didn't answer but nodded and leaned forward a little.

"I didn't want to get close to you."

I frowned. "But why? I thought you had a good relationship with my mother? Or at least loved her."

She laughed. "I loved your mother so much. She was my heart." She clasped her palm to her chest.

"Then why?"

"Like you, I lost everyone. Like you, it hurt too much to love again. Like you, I don't get too close."

"I know you lost my mom, too, but who else did you lose?"

She closed her eyes.

I waited. A feeling of dread coursed through me. As if I'd opened Pandora's Box.

"So many."

"But there was a loss greater than all the others, wasn't there?" My voice shook. Why the fuck was I pushing it?

Her eyes flew open.

"The greatest. My husband. My children."

My mouth opened in surprise. She'd been married. She'd had children. I'd had cousins.

Before I could answer, she was gone.

I heard her footsteps race down the stairs and then the front door slammed.

The next morning, she woke me at five again like normal. Like nothing had happened.

Not another word was said about losing her family.

I called James twice more. No answer. I didn't leave a message. I always called when my aunt wasn't around. I don't know why I wanted to keep it a secret.

After the third call without an answer, I called the police station to ask if he was on duty. He was. I was both relieved and morose. He was fine, but still wouldn't answer my calls or call me back. Not even a "10-4. J." to let me know he'd received my call.

Maybe he wasn't responding because I wasn't leaving a message.

Fine. I'd call back and leave a message because I missed him so much my chest hurt to think about him, and it was sometimes hard to breathe. But this time, it said his mail box was full.

That night as we got ready for bed, my aunt said she'd be leaving the next day on some top-fucking-secret mission.

"You must keep up your training. You are stronger, but you have a long way to go."

"What top-secret mission? Does it have to do with the graves? Or possible graves?"

"They were not graves."

Well, that was good to know.

"Can't you tell me where you are going? Does it have to do with King?"

She shook her head. "No, I'm sorry. Somebody else needs me. I can't help it. I must go. I don't know when I will be back. It may be a very long time."

I bit my lip. I felt inexplicably sad that I wouldn't see her every day. That the military cot she'd set up in one corner of the loft would be empty every night.

"I thought you were going to help me find King?"

"I'm sorry, Gia. I have no choice. They need me. Desperately."

"Who?" I asked. "What is it you do anyway?"

She paused and studied my face.

I held my breath. She was going to tell me.

"You know how I left you that card?"

She'd left me the queen of spades with a phone number on it. A number I'd never called. I'd been saving it. I guess for a situation like this.

I nodded.

"If someone is desperate they call me."

"Desperate? For what?"

"I have to go."

"Can't you explain? Is it top secret? What the fuck?"

"I'm sorry." She got in her cot and pulled the covers over her head.

I crawled into my own bed, stewing. Fucking secrets. I hated them.

The next morning, I woke at three and searched the dark loft for her figure on the cot. But the cot was put away. She was already gone.

30

I GOT UP AND IMMEDIATELY BEGAN MY TRAINING. BY SIX, I HAD showered and had coffee. I began searching my loft for any remnant of my aunt. Anything that showed she'd even existed. The only sign was all the healthy food in my cupboards and refrigerator. That was it.

As I searched cupboards and closets, I came across the materials for my altar to Bobby. At first, I closed the door but then I opened it back up. The Day of the Dead was only days away. I still had time to complete it to bring it to Garfield Park.

For the next three hours, I worked on the *ofrenda*.

I'd basically taped three shoe boxes together, spray painted them black and silver and used them to display photos of Bobby and me and some of the things he loved. It didn't look half bad. I'd glued small votive candles on the bottom.

Instead of making me sad to see the items Bobby had loved, it filled me with a strange feeling of hope. As if I was doing the right thing by creating this altar in his memory.

It was missing one thing, though. A cross.

Bobby was a religious guy. He didn't make a big deal about it, but he'd always talked about us getting married in a church.

And when he wasn't staying at my place, he would get up on Sundays and drive to the East Bay to go to church with his parents and sister's family.

I wanted to glue a cross to the top of his memorial. Like there would be in a church.

I didn't own a cross, though.

That's when I remembered—there was a rosary with blue stone beads in my mother's belongings. The attached cross was inlaid with intricate black, blue, and white stones.

I would use that.

After I managed to get the rosary affixed to the altar, I sat back and smiled. My mother was there, now, too. She would've loved Bobby. And James for that matter. Thinking of James wiped the smile right off my face. Carefully, I set the altar on my small table and called Tony.

———

"WE STALKING your cop boyfriend again, huh?"

"Yep. What's up with traffic today?" I asked.

People were driving like idiots. We passed two accidents on the way to the police station.

"Daylight savings."

"Is that why it's so damn dark right now?"

"People apparently forget out to drive. It's darker during the commute plus people are sleep-deprived from losing an hour of sleep. It happens every year on daylight savings."

"Is that true?"

"Ask your cop boyfriend. There are statistically more accidents on daylight savings days than others."

I totally didn't believe him but decided to keep my mouth shut. I sat back and gazed out the window.

"Plus, it's a full moon," he added.

"That I believe," I said. I knew people acted cray cray during a full moon. Even Django was acting strange today, pacing and whining for no good reason. Finally, he'd curled up on his cushion and stared at me as I got ready.

We sat in silence across the street from the police station. It was the same spot as before where we could see people coming and going out the back door.

"Where's your aunt?"

"She took off."

Silence.

"He's not much of a boyfriend, is he? I mean not if you have to do like a code four stakeout to see if he's still alive."

"Code four means everything's okay."

"Whatever."

"We had a little misunderstanding."

"Did you tell him some psycho kidnapped you and drugged you? I mean, it wasn't your fault."

I sighed. "He knows."

"Huh." Tony grunted the word.

I didn't want his sympathy, but he kept talking.

"If you were my girlfriend and someone did that to you, I wouldn't let you out of my sight."

I shrugged. I didn't feel like defending James. Probably because I couldn't.

We watched as cops came and went out the back door. One or two glanced our way. Then one guy came out the door and headed our way. *Shit.* Tony started the engine and drove away before he reached us.

Tony was pissed off. "It's a public street, right? I can park there if I want."

"Damn straight."

He dropped me off at home.

I knew the loft would feel empty without my aunt, so I

headed to Katrina's. She wasn't in, but I sat in my booth. I kept the blue velvet curtain opened and ordered a soda instead of my usual Bourbon.

"Something wrong, Gia?" the server said and gestured at my drink.

"Fuck it. The usual."

Four drinks later, I knew I'd be stumbling home. It was the absolute worst possible time to call a boyfriend or ex, but I didn't care. I gave zero fucks at that point.

Standing on the sidewalk outside Katrina's I dialed James with the burner phone my aunt had left me.

Only to be learn his number was no longer in service. Panic shot through me. What the fuck was going on? Now I was desperate enough to use my secret weapon. I'd call 911 and ask dispatch to get James a message.

"911. What is your emergency?"

"No emergency. I'm sorry to bother you. I need to get a message to Officer James Hunt"

There was a pause that made my heart stop. But her next words were worse. "I'm sorry. We have no officer by that name."

"What?"

"Ma'am, you're going to have to call the substation during regular hours."

"Please. Tell me where he is? What's going on?"

"I'm sorry, ma'am. Call the substation tomorrow. You are tying up an emergency line."

She hung up on me.

For the first time, I wished I'd gotten a phone number for his mother or aunt. Maybe he was with them or maybe they knew where he was. Would he have quit without telling me? Where was he? What if he was home in a drunken stupor because he'd been fired or something?

I bit my lip, thinking. Dispatch wasn't helpful, which wasn't a huge surprise. For all they knew I was some weird stalker chick. Then I remembered that James had once given me the inside line number at the substation. I dialed it and asked the man who answered if I could speak to Officer Hunt.

I lied and said I was his sister and that I needed to speak to him about a family emergency. The man on the other end cleared his throat.

"He's not here. I haven't seen him for a while. I heard he took a leave. Like an extended one. You don't know?"

"We haven't spoken for a while. Long story."

"Well, I'm sorry. You can call tomorrow and talk to his lieutenant. That's the only thing I can suggest."

I hung up.

Unease ran through me. This was bullshit. Something was up.

I hailed a cab and gave the driver directions to James's apartment. I didn't have time to wait for Tony.

For some reason the streets were crowded. Cars were double-parked, and people were everywhere. I didn't even pay attention, just rushed inside James's building, eager to check his apartment.

I pounded on the manager's apartment door. He didn't answer right away, so I laid on the doorbell and began kicking the door, nearly losing my balance. My buzz was wearing off, but I still felt a little unsteady.

I knew I was weaving and swaying and that it was obvious I was shitfaced, but I needed answers. Now.

A guy with a big gut hanging out of a ratty, threadbare bathrobe opened the door, blinking at the light. "Okay, okay, what the fuck? This better be an emergency."

"It is."

"Who are you?"

"I'm here about James Hunt."

"Again?" he sighed. "I would've never opened the door."

"What do you mean *again*?"

"I already gave someone my extra key to get his dog. What do you want?"

He moved to close the door. I stuck my boot between it and the doorjamb. He looked down very slowly and said, "You might want to rethink that."

That's when I noticed that he held one hand behind the door where I couldn't see it. Gun.

"Listen, I'm just worried about him." I softened my voice. "Can you let me in to his place to look around."

He glared at me.

I sighed. "I can make it worth your while." I started to reach into the inner pocket of my leather jacket, but before I could, the gun was pressing against my nose.

"Easy, tiger," I said. "You're going to like what I'm getting out." Part of me wanted to say, "If I wanted to, I'd have that gun fired into your skull before you could even release the safety. Dumb fuck." But I didn't. I wanted him on my side.

He only removed the gun when I held up a wad of cash. He ducked back into the entryway with the money clutched in his sweaty, fat fist. "Be right back."

He returned and held a key through the door. I'd barely grasped it when he slammed the door in my face. I heard a series of locks engage.

I was up the stairs in thirty seconds. My hand was trembling as I unlocked the dead bolted door. I swung it open. It was dark inside, so I reached in and flicked on some lights. A musty smell greeted me, a combination of dust and dog.

It took me about two minutes to see that something wasn't right. Mr. Neat Freak would never leave his apartment without making his bed, picking up his clothes, or running the dishwasher that now contained dirty dishes.

But as much as I searched, I found no signs of a struggle.

Think, Gia. What would James take if he was leaving but in a hurry. What are the absolute must-haves? His phone. Right. And his medicine. He had inherited high blood pressure. Even though he was a specimen of a man and in better shape than 99 percent of the cops in the SFPD, he needed medication to regulate his blood pressure.

In the bathroom, I opened the door to his mirrored medicine cabinet over the sink.

His blood pressure medicine sat right there, front and center.

That's when I knew. Wherever he was, he hadn't gone willingly.

31

AN ICY TRICKLE OF FEAR RAN ACROSS MY SCALP.

James was missing.

Tucking the key in my pocket, I locked the door behind me. I needed to think. I needed to push down the panic that was surging up my throat.

When I stepped outside, I was taken aback as I took in the crowd around me. I hadn't noticed them much before in my hurry to get into the building to find James.

Unlike me, James lived in a trendy neighborhood—the Marina. It was populated with young professionals, well-to-do artists, and older gay couples.

And tonight, they were all out in costume to celebrate Halloween.

People overflowed bars and restaurants onto the sidewalks, and I had to fight my way through the crowd to get to my place.

I passed a couple dressed as a ghoulish bride and groom with dead-white faces and blood-stained wedding garments. There were creepy clowns and devils with horns and tails. There was a Freddy Krueger and a Jason from *Friday the 13th* now that those eighties movies were back in vogue.

By the time I got to the Tenderloin, I was jumpy, walking quickly, and ready to draw my gun if I saw even a cockroach cross my path. The trepidation I'd felt realizing James was missing had been compounded by the eerily costumed party-goers filling the streets. I was ready to lock my doors and crawl into bed with Django.

The streets were dark and quiet in my neighborhood. Most people were in their places, getting ready to turn in early and wake with the sun to go to jobs scattered through the city. We didn't really have kids in the Tenderloin. And those families that did live here were smart and headed over to Nob Hill to trick or treat. We were a mix of working class residents and homeless.

Back in my place, I hugged Django to me and got on my laptop, searching for a phone number for James's mother or aunt. I struck out.

I dialed Danny.

"You think you could find a phone number for these women?" I said and gave him the names.

"I'll give it a shot."

My night was awful. I couldn't sleep, waking every hour, sick with worry about James. I knew the only thing that would burn off my anxiety, or at least bring it down to a manageable level, was an intense work out. I got up early and dressed in clothes to go workout with Kato.

On my way to the Dojo, I parked my motorcycle at the building where Danny had seen the drone land. When I called this morning to see if he'd found numbers for James's mother or aunt, I got his voice mail. I knew he was probably sleeping. The kid was nocturnal. Most of the time, that came in handy. Today it was just irritating.

The homeless guy wasn't there, which also bothered me. Did the absence of his lookout mean that King had cleared out? I started my bike and left.

Having Kato work me out—sparring and kicking and punching until I was dripping sweat—was good for me and helped relieve some of my unease. But I needed to talk, too. Kato was also a friend.

"Something is wrong," I said, when we took a break. I explained what was going on with James. I leaned against the wall and used a small white towel to wipe my brow.

"It doesn't sound good," Kato said.

"I don't know what to do."

"File a missing person's report?"

"They laughed at me."

I'd called earlier and said that my boyfriend was a police officer there and that he was missing. When I said I wanted to file a missing person's report, I was connected to a sergeant:

"Cavanaugh."

"My boyfriend, Officer James Hunt is missing. He left his apartment without telling me. He didn't take his important medicine with him. I'd like to report him missing."

"Hold please."

After a few seconds, he got back on the phone "You're welcome to come file a report, but my lieutenant said it's going to be low priority. We show Officer Hunt as requesting a leave of absence for the next six months."

Six months? My heart sunk.

"That doesn't mean anything," I said. "If he was leaving town, he would've taken his blood pressure medicine."

"Who knows? I mean, maybe he swung by the pharmacy and picked up a new bottle on his way out of town?"

I hung up without even saying thank you and mulled over what the sergeant had said.

It was possible. Unlikely, but possible. But I could check. So, I'd gone back to his place, grabbed his prescription bottle and examined it. There was one refill left. I dialed the automated number and was allowed to refill it. That meant James hadn't refilled shit before he disappeared.

I told Kato all of this.

"What can I do?" His brow was wrinkled in concern. I was so lucky to count him as a friend.

"I wish I knew," I said.

"I'm sorry, Gia."

There was nothing else to say.

Back at my place, I eyed the altar that took center stage on my kitchen table. Tomorrow was the Day of the Dead. Even though I was so anxious with worry about James that I wanted to curl up in the fetal position, I vowed to stick with my plan to bring Bobby's altar to Garfield Park and participate in the *Dia de los Muertos* ceremonies.

Despite everything, I knew I needed to let Bobby go. That way when—*not if*—but when I saw James again, I'd be ready to give him everything I had.

32

AFTER NOT SLEEPING MUCH ALL NIGHT, I FINALLY CLOSED MY EYES at dawn and slept until one in the afternoon.

It was *Dia de los Muertos.*

At least I had something to do today. Instead of being excited about it, I felt lethargic—heavy, like I was sinking in molasses. But I was determined to go through with it.

While it was still light out, I joined dozens of others at Garfield park setting up their altars. I couldn't very well drive my motorcycle while holding on to it, so I took the city bus. I'd called Tony. But he was caught up in a ride to the San Jose airport. Sitting on the bus, I got a few nods of approval from people, but mostly I was ignored. I'd have to do something much weirder than holding a two-by-two-foot boxed structure for anyone to give me a second glance in San Francisco.

I walked the park twice before I found a spot I thought Bobby would like. It was deep in the heart of the park under a small tree. Several other altars were already placed there. Some altars were as big as my bathroom—elaborate creations they must've used a truck to bring in.

I decided to put Bobby between an older man's and a

teenage girl's altar. The man's altar had photos of him with a large family and a black-and-white Navy picture that showed him as a handsome young man. The teenage girl's altar had photos showing her standing by a bright red Jeep with some other teenagers. One picture was of her at a dance wearing a pink dress.

I put Bobby's altar down smack between the two, figuring they looked friendly. I stood up, uncertain. Was this it? What now? I looked around to see what other people were doing. Mostly people stood in clumps talking. I decided to go home. Tonight, after the procession, I'd have my own personal conversation with Bobby at his altar. I'd tell him I was sorry once and for all and let him go.

I was doing all of this for myself, but also for James, fervently grasping to the slim thread of hope that he was okay and would be home soon. The thought of endless days and nights unrolling before me without knowing where he might be was too much to handle. I stomped those dark thoughts down and tried to concentrate on being in the moment.

Now, my goal was to say my goodbyes to Bobby so that when James returned home—if he still wanted me—I'd be ready for him. I decided to walk home from the park. It was still hours before the sunset procession would begin.

At home, I'd attempt to eat something even though my stomach was a roiling mess, maybe drink a bottle of wine, and then get dressed in my costume before returning for the procession. Darling told me many people wore costumes, so I'd picked out a Catrina outfit online. It had arrived this morning. I'd be dressed like a dead woman, and I was okay with that. After all, if I was going to do this, I was doing it all the way. I've never been a halfway type of girl.

When I got to my building, the front door was propped open. I looked around warily. All my tenants knew I was strict about the building's security. That's when I looked down and saw what was keeping the door open: Thanh-Thanh's familiar New Yorker tote bag with a stack of mail spilling out of it.

I rushed to my friend's apartment on the second floor. Her door was wide open. I took my gun out of my waistband and stepped to the side, slowly making my way in. I'd only taken a few steps when I heard her moan. Thanh-Thanh was crumpled in the corner by the window holding a towel to her cheek. Blood oozed from the corner of her eye. She met my gaze with her other big brown eye. Her pink, Cupid's-bow lips crumpled as she wept.

Oh my God.

I raced over. "Are you okay?"

She was crying too hard to speak. I grabbed my phone and dialed 911.

"Send an ambulance. Someone broke in and attacked my friend."

I hung up and took Thanh-Thanh's chin, lifting it. Her eye was bloodshot but intact. A small cut to the side of it bled profusely. I examined her pupils. They were dilated. She'd received a bad blow and probably had a concussion. I patted her back.

"You're going to be okay. Who did this?"

"A big guy. A man with white hair was with him."

King.

I was going to kill that son of a bitch.

"The big ma was bald. He hit me with my Buddha statue. The white-haired man said he wanted me to give you a message."

"I'm so sorry." I closed my eyes. Once again, someone I cared about had been hurt because of me. This was going to stop. And it was going to stop soon. "What message?"

"He said to call the number on my phone." She lifted her

chin, pointing to a cell phone sitting on the armrest of her couch.

I grabbed the phone and dialed the last number I saw.

"I have him."

King had James. My stomach dropped. "I'll kill you."

He laughed.

"I'm proposing an exchange."

"What do you want?"

"What I've always wanted."

"Please enlighten me."

"You. You seem to forget. You are mine."

"Whatever." It wasn't worth arguing with an insane person.

"We can arrange to meet—"

I cut him off. "Meet me at Garfield Park at eight. As soon as I see that James is safe and released, I'll go with you. I'll go wherever you want."

And I would, too. King had succeeded. He'd driven me to surrender. I'd go with him. I'd do anything to stop him from hurting the people I cared about. But I'd also use every second I was with him to try to kill him. That, I vowed with every ounce of my being.

33

Everyone scattered as the gunshots rang out across Garfield Park. I'd run toward James and was in the dirt holding his head in my lap.

I was screaming something—*Get an ambulance. Call 911. Get help*—when I was yanked from the ground and thrown against a tree by someone with ungodly strength. That's when I realized. These cops *were* 911. We were fucked.

I tried to stand, but my legs buckled and I collapsed again. A bulky officer stood over James and pointed his gun at him saying loudly, "I told you to drop the gun!"

I watched in horror. The gun glinted in candlelight off to one side. Way out of James's reach. The officer shouted again. "Drop the gun or I'll shoot!"

I didn't understand. He was going to kill him. In cold blood. Murder him outright. Assassinate him. I screamed just as some officers who had gone after King and his men returned.

The bulky cop startled.

"What are you doing?" one officer said, touching the arm of the amped up cop.

The officer lowered his gun and seemed flustered. "I thought I saw him holding a gun."

"It's okay, man. It's okay. The gun's over here."

The officer kicked James in the side but backed off and put his gun away. I heard James groan. I was about to run over when someone said, "Hey, where'd the girl go?"

I shrank into shadows, ducking behind a tree.

The bulky cop searched the tree where he'd thrown me.

"Let's find her."

Just then, two EMTs ran up with flashlights. I hadn't heard the sirens—they must've been parked nearby in case something went wrong in the crowd.

"It's Hunt."

I exhaled in relief. Someone recognized him. Someone who wasn't a lunatic cop about to assassinate him.

"You okay, buddy?"

I heard James groan and say, "I been better."

I'd never been so happy to hear his voice in my life.

"We're going to take care of you," the same voice said.

Meanwhile the other officers were panicking, all speaking at once.

"Jesus Christ!"

"Motherfucker."

"You shot a damn cop, Smith."

"He had a gun pointed at me."

"We need to get Internal Affairs out here ASAP."

"Officer-involved shooting at Garfield Park. We shot one of our own."

I used the distraction as a chance to crawl toward the crowd. I blended in, casting a glance back. Something was very, very wrong. And the police were suddenly the bad guys. If they arrested me, I was fucked. I needed to stay free to hunt down King and find out what was going on. It went against all my instincts, but I had to leave James.

The paramedics would take care of him. I'd heard his voice. He was alive. The worst of the danger was over. I hoped.

There was nothing I could do here right now.

I had to go after King before he was in the wind once more. I'd let him go once. I wasn't going to let him go again. He'd never stop hunting me, so I needed to *hunt* him. Stop him. For good.

34

I wanted to change out of my bloody Catrina outfit, but the most I'd done was rip the skirt at the knees while I was on the bus. A junkie nodding off across the aisle sat up for a second when he heard the taffeta ripping, but then slumped back into his stupor.

My blood was pumping when I hopped off the bus a block away from the building Danny had tracked to drone to. It was my only lead. I didn't know where else to go. Although my white-painted face probably glowed in the dark, I still kept to the shadows as I made my way closer.

From across the street, I saw the homeless guy still hadn't returned to his post.

I passed by and didn't cross the street until I was out of eyeshot. Then I took a side street so I could come up on the back of the building.

The neighborhood was quiet. All the lights were out in the apartment buildings and the only sound was the distant bleat of a foghorn. A few streets away, the bus had rolled through some low fog. It was heading my way.

I could see small wisps and strands floating on the ocean-scented breeze.

Just then, a small drone appeared before me.

"Jesus H. Christ!" I screamed and jumped.

It was the tiniest drone I'd ever seen. It looked like a mini helicopter the size of my palm. It hovered a few feet in front of me, bouncing up and down like an excited puppy.

It started to rift off, then returned again before flying a few feet away. It was as if it wanted me to follow it. It had to be Danny.

I dialed his number.

"Yo. I got something for you."

"Talk to me."

"King was there tonight. Like 30 minutes ago."

"Okay."

"They went to Albion Castle."

"What? I have no idea what that is? Is it in San Francisco?"

"Hunter's Point."

Oh. The area where city buses had to have police escorts. Terrific.

"I'll text you the address. A few years back, it was supposed to be converted into a brewery, but then the new owner died in a freak accident in Hawaii before construction began."

"What kind of freak accident." I looked around me, uneasily.

"Got caught in an underwater cave while snorkeling."

I swallowed. If anything gave me claustrophobia it was the thought of being trapped underground. Trapped underground *and* underwater? Yeah, I'd probably go into cardiac arrest before I ran out of oxygen.

"Thanks. I'm on my way."

I hung up and the drone took off.

TONY LAUGHED when he pulled up.

"What are you supposed to be?"

"Fuck off."

But as we drove to Hunter's Point, every once in a while, he'd look over at me and snicker until finally I said, "I'm a Catrina."

"A what what?"

"Do you know anything about *Dia de los Muertos*?" I tried to sound snotty.

"*Nada, amiga.*"

I gave him a fake glare.

We pulled into the Hunter's Point area and headed for a warehouse district. Then, in the middle of this industrial area, right between Innes Avenue and Northridge Road, was what looked to be a small park. The large trees and plants seemed incongruous among the gray buildings on each side. The vegetation was so thick I couldn't see past it to the structure inside. A metal gate barred entry.

Tony parallel parked right in front of the gate.

"Here you go, milady."

I had my hand on the door handle, but hesitated.

"You gonna wait for me?"

"I don't know," he said, looking pointedly at the blood on my dress. "Am I going to be an accomplice to a crime?"

I remembered he was on probation. "Go on home. I'll be fine."

He tilted his head and examined my eyes. "You sure."

I stared back. "Positive. I handed him a one-hundred-dollar bill. Have a good night. Go spend some quality time with your wife."

"Girlfriend."

"Whatever. Your woman. But first will you give me a boost over the gate?"

He laughed. "Sure."

I stood on his gnarled hands, and he lifted me up so that I was able to get one knee over the top. I straddled the gate before dropping softly to the dirt on the other side, landing almost gracefully on my hands and knees. Standing, I brushed myself off.

"You good?"

"Thanks, Tony. Talk soon."

"Hey, that wasn't real blood on you, was it?"

I didn't answer, just turned toward the building before me.

The brick structure loomed amongst the trees. The first story was covered in vines and brush, but a rectangular brick tower soared high above the rest of the structure. Wide stone steps led to a wooden door. When I reached the steps, I saw the door was propped open about a foot. A tiny key box was attached to the railing nearby.

I nudged the thick door open a little with my foot and stepped back. Cool air streamed out from the entryway and made all the tiny hairs on my arms stand up straight. It carried the faint scent of salt water. I reached down to my ankle and released my dagger from its sheath. I held it in front of me.

My phone buzzed. It was Danny. I damn near jumped through the roof.

I stepped to the side into the cover of shadows. "Yes?" I whispered, casting a fearful glance at the entrance to the castle.

"I just found out the castle is for rent—long-term only."

That explained where King has been holed up. Right here. Figures that King would want to live in a damn castle. Megalomaniac.

"I'm almost in."

"There are tunnels underneath. An underground aquifer. Cisterns."

"Anything else?" I whispered.

"Be careful. Also, I'm watching you."

The small white helicopter drone was suddenly off to my side.

I hung up and stepped inside. The place was dark, but the full moon streaming through high windows made it easy to see clumps of furniture. Carefully, I headed toward a hall. The house was dark and quiet.

As I stepped into the hall, I heard the whir of the drone behind me. It comforted me that Danny was watching, but what could the drone do to help? Nothing.

Moonlight poured out of each room lining the hall. Which meant all the doors were open. I peeked inside each one individually. A few were bedrooms with neatly made beds. One was an office. One was a bathroom.

That's when I heard a door close.

I wasn't alone.

35

I SILENTLY CREPT TOWARD THE NOISE. OFF THE KITCHEN THERE was a massive wooden door. Like the front door, it stood open as if waiting for me. A chill ran through me. The coldness trickling out of that yawning blackness beyond seemed to seep into my bones.

I heard footsteps then, coming from the dark doorway. Someone was running down steps.

Any hesitation was gone. With one hand holding the dagger before me and the other grasping for a handrail, I stepped inside the doorway. My feet found the stairs and my hand closed around a bar leading into the darkness. Keeping to one side, I made my way down the stairway. About ten steps in, I must've rounded a corner because a dim light shone far below.

I quickened my pace. At the bottom, I paused as my eyes adjusted to the light. I was in a stone cavern, and could smell and hear water. The eerie, shimmering light on the rough rock walls reflected moving water. I stepped inside and saw the cave was lit with rudimentary bulbs strung on the wall. Across from me was a waist-high wall with turquoise water lapping at its edge under a coved ceiling—a cistern containing water from the aquifer.

There were three of these cisterns in the cave. Between two of them another dark doorway stood ominously. I thought I sensed movement there.

"Hiding in the dark isn't going to save you," I said.

That's when King's laughter rolled out, echoing across the vast cavern.

"Standing in the light will kill you." As he spoke I ducked back into the stairway doorway as a bullet struck the wall beside me. Another bullet struck the wall inside my alcove, showering me with jagged stone shrapnel. My hearing was gone.

Instead of retreating up the stairs, I ducked and stayed pressed to one side, hoping I'd get lucky and the angle would prevent him from getting off an accurate shot. Then again, with my luck, I'd probably take a ricochet to the throat.

I heard shuffling and realized he'd left his hiding spot. I peeked out and saw that right outside the door was a light switch. *Unbelievable.*

As I hit the switch, plunging us into darkness, I saw King coming in fast from off to the left. I immediately dropped to the floor and Army-crawled to the right, toward the closest cistern. Within seconds, I'd hauled myself up on the small wall and slid into the water without a sound. I was relieved there hadn't been a splash.

The water was icy cold. I stifled a gasp. My heart was racing from the shock of the sudden drop in body temperature. My limbs instantly started to numb and my hands hurt from the cold. I reminded myself to never take part in a polar plunge. Dante had told me people actually did this sort of shit for fun in the Midwest in the middle of winter. Nope.

I clutched the dagger frantically under water. It was my only hope.

My feet, thank God, touched the bottom of the cistern. If I'd have had to tread water, the gig would've been up since the noise would've alerted King to my hiding place. But the chill of the water was already taking a toll. I only allowed my head to crest the surface from the nose up, so I could breathe and see over the top of the short wall, keeping an eye on the direction where I'd last seen King.

I knew I'd made the right move when I saw a light flicker on across the cavern.

King was using his cell phone to illuminate the space in front of him as he walked.

"Come out, come out, wherever you are. It's just you and me now, Gia. I don't want to hurt you. I want you as my own. I've rarely met a woman like you. You just don't quit. You are powerful—more powerful than you even realize."

I could feel my face scrunch in confusion. That's when I remembered that vague hazy memory of the first night I'd been given his new drug. He'd been caressing me and whispering sweet nothings. And I'd responded, not knowing it was him. I felt filthy. Disgusting. Sick to my stomach.

He was making his way toward me, keeping to the edge of the cave with his back to the wall while shining his light in front of him. The light, however, didn't penetrate to the center of the cave. This meant he kept his eyes glued toward the middle. Soon, he would be backing up to me. Right where I wanted him.

The hand holding my dagger underwater was growing weaker. Slowly, so as not to cause a ripple, I raised it so it was near the surface. I kept my eye on King.

When his back hit the small wall, he jumped a little, making the beam of light from his phone jiggle, but quickly regained his composure. He inched his way along the wall, growing closer.

Holding my breath, I lifted the hand clasping the dagger out of the water ever so slowly, praying it didn't make a sound. But then he was right there in front of me. Throwing caution to the wind, I burst out of the water before he was able to turn around. I looped my arm around his throat and pressed the razor edge to his neck. My mouth was at his ear. He dropped the gun and phone. Both clattered loudly to the cave floor. The phone landed so the flashlight shone up on the ceiling.

"DON'T PRETEND that you love me, King. You didn't even think twice about using me as a subject in your sick experiments," I said in a low voice with my lips near his ear.

He smelled like cologne and shampoo. He smelled expensive. I'd expected him to smell putrid somehow, like death. The death that he'd wrought across my city. I could feel the blood pulsing in his neck by my mouth.

"Do it," was all he said.

But I hesitated. I'd killed before in a fit of blind rage. But that slaying was justified. That man had killed Bobby. He'd also killed my parents. Killing him was done without thought or remorse. I couldn't live another second knowing he walked the earth.

This man had tried to kill my dog. He'd beaten my sweet friend, Thanh-Thanh. He'd murdered Layla and countless others over the years. He had to die. It was my duty to do so.

I pressed the blade harder to his throat. "Keep your hands still."

I'd felt movement from him. But something prevented me from slicing his throat open. I whispered in his ear. "Why would you risk everything to come after me? I don't buy that you *want* me."

"You killed Benny."

I nearly dropped the dagger at his words.

Benny was the man who'd raped me while I was a teenager in Monterey. My sensei, Jun's, son.

It didn't make sense. How had they even known each other?

Then it struck me. The eyes were the same. That's what I'd subconsciously realized at the clinic. "He was your brother."

I remembered that Jun had mentioned that Benny had a stepbrother. His mother had remarried a Norwegian man.

At the same time, I said the words, I heard a whirring sound. The drone.

The distraction was enough for him. With my focus drawn to the drone, I'd let up on the pressure and King managed to slip a fist between my forearm and his throat, thrusting the blade away. At the same time, he spun and sunk his teeth into my neck. Before I could react, he was in the water on top of me. I was able to gasp for air right before he pushed my head underwater with seemingly inhuman strength.

My limbs flailed. I tried to fight back, to punch and kick, but I was already so weak from sitting in the ice-cold water. Panicking, I pushed against him with all my strength. But he was stronger and outweighed me. He had both hands on my head holding me down.

I was going to die.

I needed air. Every cell in my body screamed for oxygen. I wasn't strong enough. I was going to open my mouth to gasp and that would be it.

But just as I thought this, the pressure released. I soared to the surface in time to see King lurch out of the cistern and chase after the drone. It had a small spotlight and camera. Danny had been filming my murder. *Evidence.*

King was trying to snag the contraption out of the air. The drone swooped in and then zipped away at the last second. They were across the cavern now. I hauled myself over the small wall and dropped to the cave floor feeling around for King's gun. My hand closed on the cold steel at the same moment King's foot landed a kick to my head. I reeled from the blow but managed to pull the trigger aiming into the air above me. I kept firing until the chamber was emptied.

Danny adjusted the drone, shining its light on the small wall keeping the water at bay.

King was slumped against it, eyes unseeing. His chest covered in dark red blood.

36

Sitting in the waiting room, I had my head in my hands. I was dressed in men's clothes. Tony had made me change into some of his old jeans and a flannel shirt. When I walked out of the gate of the castle's gate, soaking wet and shaking like a leaf, his car had been waiting. He'd given me a wry smile.

The clothes were warm and dry, but my hair was still dripping wet. I was shivering, but all I could do was pray for James. I was pleading with the God my mother had so fervently believed in.

Please spare his life. Please save James.

Meanwhile, James's mother and aunt were across the room. I could tell they were praying, as well.

When the surgeon came out, he walked straight over to them and I rushed over to hear what he had to say. He raised an eyebrow at me, but didn't wave me away.

"The surgery was difficult. There was a moment or two there that took a few years off my life."

I gasped, but nobody looked at me.

"The surgery was successful in that it saved his life, stopping internal bleeding." He paused.

Relief flooded me, but I was frozen waiting for him to continue. I knew there was a "but" coming and I wasn't mistaken.

"But the most damage was an injury to the C1 vertebrae," he said. "It's highly unlikely that he'll regain movement in his lower limbs. However, it is an incomplete injury so nothing is set in stone. Time will tell."

I started to have tunnel vision. My face felt icy. The doctor's words zoomed in and out.

James's aunt burst into tears. His mother closed her eyes for a long second and then opened them again and said, "He's not going to walk?"

The doctor pursed his lips and cast his gaze to the floor. "It's doubtful. I'm very sorry there wasn't more we could do."

My insides were hollow. James was paralyzed. Thank God he was alive, though. I nearly cried from the sheer relief that he'd survived, but I was sick about him losing the loss of his legs. How would he take it? What would it do to him? He was such a strong, vibrant, athletic person. All these thoughts raced through my head.

"He's in recovery," the doctor said. "I'll come get you when he wakes."

Who would tell him? I wondered with horror.

His mother must've thought the same thing. "Are you going to tell him? Straight away?"

The doctor pressed his lips together tightly. "It depends."

"Can I tell him?" she said. Her voice was small. "Can I tell my boy?"

It was one of the bravest things I'd ever heard. I held my breath, waiting for the doctor to answer. He simply nodded.

"I'll come get you when he wakes."

His mother stood and grabbed her handbag. "We're going to

the chapel," she said to the doctor. "If we aren't here when you come out, can you send someone to get us?"

"I'll come get you," I said.

But she ignored me, staring at the doctor until he said yes.

I sat with my head in my hands trying to process what the doctor had said. All I wanted to do was see James and his warm smile, but I was worried sick that he wouldn't be smiling. That he might never smile again. That he would be a different James, bitter and angry about the loss of his legs. And I couldn't blame him.

His mother and aunt had returned by the time the doctor came out.

"He's awake. I told him the three of you were here."

I felt a surge of gratefulness to this man. For saving James's life but also for including me.

"I'll wait here until you are done," I told his mother. She ignored me, but the aunt gave me a small nod not soaked in pure disdain.

Wanting to weep and wail, I tore at my hair a little while I was waiting. It took all my willpower not to run down the hall and burst into the room I'd seen them go into. It seemed like forever until they came out again.

When they first emerged, they didn't see me.

His mother collapsed against one wall, tears pouring down her face. Her sister patted her arm and handed her a handkerchief. I felt guilty seeing such an intimate scene. His mother didn't appear to be the type to show her emotions in public.

She noticed me standing there and immediately stood up straight.

I walked over with trepidation. "How is he?"

She looked away. "He's never going to be the same again."

Hearing the words out loud shocked me. I didn't know what to say.

"Maybe you should leave? Just leave him alone," Her voice grew shrill, and she shot a glance back at the door to James's room, lowering her voice. "Haven't you done enough?"

I shook my head fiercely and pointed at the door. "That's not...I didn't...that wasn't..." *My fault.* Or was it? I took a deep breath. I had to be calm. Mature. Logical.

"I love your son. I would do anything to spare him this pain. I would give my life for his," I said. Tears blurred my vision and I had to swallow to continue. "If that isn't what every mother wants for her son, then I don't know what to tell you. It's everything I have. It's all I am. If that's not enough, then we have nothing more to say."

His mother threw back her shoulders and lifted her chin.

"He was just fine before you came along."

I scoffed. "Really?" He was lonely. He sat at home eating alone every night."

"He had me," she said through clenched teeth.

"Sorry, but you're not enough." I shook my head in frustration. Did she want me to fucking spell it out for her? "I'm sorry to break the news but he is not your little boy anymore. He's a grown man. And he needs a woman. And I believe that I'm that woman—whether you like me or not. I'm in his life and I'm going to stay there."

Her sister, James's aunt, was tugging on her arm. "Come on, let's go now."

His mother was shaking a little and I couldn't help but feel bad for her, but I'd needed to say it. Every. Word.

"I know I don't fit your idea of the perfect woman for James. I'm not as educated or refined or well, hell, polite as you ladies. Not to mention the fact that I'm white." There. I had to get it out there. I'd been insecure about it from day one. And if that's why she didn't like me, that was the lamest reason on earth.

His aunt started laughing.

"What?" I whirled on her.

"Our mama was white." She gave me a genuine smile, but I sat there stunned.

I was taken aback. James had never told me this. But then again, why would he have needed to? "Well, um, then, whatever. You don't like me, and I don't know why."

"I don't want you to hurt my boy."

"Listen..." It was his aunt. "We only want what's best for James."

That made me angry. "What if I'm what's best?"

His mother's eyes were shiny with tears. "I know your type."

"What the fuck does that mean?" I'd been trying not to drop the f-bomb in front of these refined women, but she'd gone too far.

"You are far too selfish to stay with and care for a cripple."

Anger surged through me, and I clenched my fists, biting out my words. "You don't know me. And I hope to God you never use that word around your son."

"What about when you want babies?" she said. "You'll leave him for someone who can give you a family."

Her voice was so sad that all of my anger seeped out of me. Tears sprung to my eyes. James wanted a family. He wanted to be a father. Me? I wasn't sure about kids, but the realization that something James had dreamed of was now possibly impossible for him now felt like a punch to my gut.

"I already told you where I stand on that. That I won't ever hurt him." Again.

"I believe that's what you think. That's what you believe. That may even be what you want," she said. "But I don't believe that's what's going to happen."

I opened my mouth to respond but nothing came out. Not a word. She stared at me for a few seconds and then turned and left. I watched them walk down the hospital hallway and it wasn't until they rounded the corner that I realized I had tears streaming down my face.

37

As soon as I got my shit together, I rushed into the room and to James. Seeing his face filled me with joy. He smiled and damn it, I started crying again. He had a brace on his neck and tubes connected to machines everywhere. He couldn't even lift his head.

"I wanted to come see you right away, but I let your mama come first. Waiting to see you was one of the hardest things I've ever done."

He smiled. "Thank you."

Then couldn't resist it, I leaned forward and kissed his forehead and his cheek and his mouth. He kissed me back hungrily.

But I was worried and pulled back. "Oh James. I'm so damn sorry. For everything."

"Not your fault."

"Tell your mama that."

"It'll be fine."

I shook my head.

"I supposed you heard what the doctor said..." I was fighting with all my strength to keep my tears at bay.

"Yes."

He took my hand and squeezed it tightly. "None of that matters right now."

I nodded. "I'm just so grateful you're alive."

There was so much I wanted to say: we can figure this out, we can work through this. But I also felt like I didn't have the right to say any of that. I was barely his girlfriend. I wasn't his wife. And I wasn't the one who was probably paralyzed.

"That's not what I meant."

I froze.

"The reason all this happened to me," he said. "Is because I was betrayed. The police department is corrupt, Gia. They were colluding with King. They basically handed me over to him."

"*What?* What are you talking about?"

"When you disappeared, I started to suspect that King had an in to the department because when I went to report you missing I was totally blown off. Then I was taken aside and told that I should never mention King's name again if I knew what was good for me. That the last officer who'd tried to open an investigation into King ended up shot dead while on patrol."

I just shook my head. But then I looked around and whispered. "You don't have to worry about that anymore. He's dead."

His eyes widened. I held my finger over his lips. "Sshhh."

"To protect you—well to protect us—and still dig around, I made a big deal out of saying I didn't think you'd actually disappeared, that I thought you dumped me. That's also why I never answered your calls. I didn't trust that they weren't monitoring my cell phone. I didn't trust them at all. That's why I stayed away. I'm sorry."

I swallowed and nodded. He'd been trying to keep me safe.

"But I couldn't come up with anything and I think they started to catch on that I was still looking. They forced me to take a leave. My sergeant told me that I should spend the time looking for a new job. Far away from here if I wanted to stay on this side of the dirt."

"Those fuckers." I didn't know what else to say so I just stared.

"But guess what?" he said in a steel tone of voice I'd never heard before.

I raised an eyebrow.

"You and me? We're going to go after them. We are going to expose every last corrupt officer in the department, do you understand?"

His face suddenly looked strained, and then he grimaced. The monitor on the other side of the bed showed lines bobbing furiously. He needed to calm down.

"Do you understand?"

"Yes," I said. "Yes. I'll do anything you want. We'll find out who did this to you. And we'll make them pay."

"Good." He clenched his jaw, and he relaxed his head into the pillow. His monitors slowly returned to a more normal pace.

The emotion appeared to have exhausted him. He turned slightly away from me, and his eyes fluttered.

"Why don't you try to sleep?" I said. "I'll be right here. I'm not going anywhere."

He didn't answer, but before long, his breathing slowed and his chest rose and fell rhythmically. He was asleep.

EPILOGUE

The feel of the Boeing 747 racing down the runway, pressing me into my seat, gave me a thrill that few things could. It never got old.

As soon as we leveled out, the guy beside me, who'd been white-knuckling the armrests, turned to me and started talking about why he was going to Cuba. I smiled politely but then dug out my backpack from under the seat in front of me. A silk zip-up bag inside contained my airplane emergency kit. It served two purposes—to repel chatty seatmates and to let me thoroughly relax. I smiled as I pulled out a bottle of water, my noise-canceling headphones and my eye mask. I set the mask on my lap, hoping the guy would take the hint since it was black with white letters that said, "Fuck Off."

But first, before I slept, I would take in the view. I could never resist the sight of my beloved city from the air. The sun had nearly set. The sky was brilliant orange, red, and pink and the skyscrapers glowed, reflecting the myriad colors. To my left, the Golden Gate bridge lived up to its name and then to my right, the top of Mt. Tamalpais gleamed like an emerald.

I gazed in wonder at the beauty of San Francisco. It had

captured my heart since I was a little girl and my mother had first brought me here from Monterey to show me its wonders.

We did a giant swooping turn, a gentle curving motion as we turned around over the ocean and began to head south. I knew somewhere below were all the people I loved. Those still alive and those who had died.

Bobby's body was under ground and his spirit was forever lost to me, but I was at peace. He'd let me go. I don't know how or why, but I was finally free of the guilt that had threatened to destroy me.

I'd avenged my parents. I'd avenged all the innocents that King had murdered. They'd found Nichelle and Dania's bodies floating alongside the Dragon Lady's in one of the cisterns under Albion Castle. I didn't ask if it was the same pool of water I'd been in. I couldn't.

James and I still were going after the police department. Right now, they didn't view him as a threat—a fired and para- lyzed police officer. But they'd underestimated him. When I returned from Cuba next week, we'd make a plan. James urged me to go to Cuba to help Dante, telling me that he'd be fine. He was visiting his mother for the week.

I called Tony to drive me to the airport. James had come along for the ride. He'd only been released from the hospital the day before. He was just getting used to manipulating a wheel- chair. He had control from the waist up, and the doctors said they were so surprised by that, that anything was possible—that he might regain use of his legs with time and physical therapy.

If anyone could do it through sheer strength and willpower alone, it would be James.

He said he wanted to practice getting in and out of the car on his own. At the airport, he came with me to the security gate, and he kissed me goodbye, telling me he would miss me more than I knew. And that his mother had invited me to her Pacific Heights house for dinner when I returned.

"You're kidding me, right?"

He smiled. *Damn it.* I was fighting back tears again. What was wrong with me lately?

And then I surprised myself even more by saying I'd go. I'd do anything for that man. If it meant dinner with his mother, I'd be there. If it meant him smiling like that? Well, fuck yeah, I'd be there. I thought back to how brave she'd been in the hospital. How she'd volunteered to tell James about his legs. She was a tough lady. I respected the hell out of that.

Because she needed to know I wasn't going anywhere. I wasn't going to leave her son. And I wasn't going to leave this city.

This was my city. This was my home.

And I'd do anything to protect it and the people who lived here.

King was gone, but I was sure some other evil would soon appear in my city.

I'd be ready.

The story continues in *Border Line*, the next Gia Santella Thriller. Head to the next page for a sneak peek or scan the QR code below to order today!

Stay up to date with Kristi Belcamino's new releases by scanning the QR code below!
(You'll receive a **free** copy of *First Vengeance: A Gia Santella Prequel!*)

Did you enjoy *Day of the Dead*? Scan the QR code below to let us know your thoughts!

BORDER LINE CHAPTER 1

The red glow of taillights illuminated the windshield. There was a seemingly endless stream of cars in front of us lumbering down Mission Street.

I couldn't believe how trendy the Mission had become. Used to be you could zip over and grab a burrito with the locals. Now I had to jockey with white kids from the suburbs trying to navigate narrow city streets looking for a place to clog up traffic in their clumsy amateur attempts to parallel park.

Despite the invasion from the suburbs, the Mission was still the best place to find authentic, delicious Mexican food—even if you had to wait in line with tourists from every country under the sun and a bevy of rich people slumming from the East Bay.

I was mainly irritated because I couldn't find a place to park my Jeep. Had it just been me, I would've taken my motorcycle, but James was with me. We needed the Jeep and its special accommodations. I wanted to park close to the restaurant so he didn't have to navigate the crowds in his wheelchair, but I knew he'd be angry with me for thinking that. And the truth was, he did just fine on his own. It'd only been a few months since he'd been injured, but he already handled the wheelchair like a pro, even giving me a slight heart attack when he took it down some stairs once.

"There," James said and pointed at a car a block away from the taqueria. I squinted and then noticed the backup lights flicker on.

I slammed on the brakes. The drivers behind me honked, and I was tempted to stick my finger out the window but smiled instead. It was a beautiful day. It was Saturday so we didn't have to work, and I was with the man I loved about to fill my belly with the food I loved. The only food I craved more was Cuban. I'd been back from visiting Dante in Cuba for a month, but still hankered for some *ropa vieja*. Dante had been in Havana doing research for his new Cuban restaurant and promised that when he began testing out the recipes he'd drop some by for me and James. I couldn't wait.

When the small white car pulled out, I slipped into the spot.

"Damn, girl, where'd you learn to parallel park?" James said, winking.

I shrugged. "Oh, some cop I know taught me."

As soon as I said it I froze. James was no longer a cop. He never talked about it. Instead, he threw himself into his new business as a private investigator. He'd taken on a few clients since he'd left the hospital and rehab—mostly people he'd known as a cop. But his main case was bringing the corrupt cops in the San Francisco Police Department down. The ones responsible for him being in a wheelchair. When he stayed over at my loft, I'd often wake in the middle of the night and catch him at the kitchen table, scouring websites on his laptop—searching and researching and hunting—trying to connect the dots.

"There's a paper trail somewhere. I just know it," he'd say.

Someone in his department had given James up to one of the evilest men I'd ever met. Kraig King had been the national head of the country's largest white supremacist group. He'd taken over our neighborhood once, preying on the homeless and stuffing their bodies in massive vats of acid to dissolve. After going into hiding when I went after him, he'd returned last year as part of an evil plan with a crooked doctor trying to find a cure for opiate addiction at the expense of young homeless women's lives. That's when we had our run-in, and King ended up dead.

But before that, King had arranged a hit on James at the hands of the dirty cops on the force. His plan had failed, but James had been shot and paralyzed.

We knew the Chief of Police was in on it, and my idea was just to take him out, but I knew James would never forgive me for that. He wanted the chief to go down publicly, and legally, and to rot in prison. Which wasn't the worst idea ever.

While James dug up dirt on the chief, I tried to tamp down my blood thirst toward the crooked cop.

I waited on the sidewalk now for James to maneuver himself into his wheelchair. It took all my willpower to sit back and not help.

Having James—my big, strong, buff-cop boyfriend—disabled, had taught me a lot the past few months. Mainly that I was a control freak. But also, that it was possible to have screaming fights with a man I loved and then make up and stay together.

In the past, I would've ghosted at the first sign of conflict. Now I stuck around.

And it was worth it.

Most of our arguments stemmed from James learning how to navigate the world on his own as a disabled person and me allowing him to do it. On. His. Own.

It wasn't easy.

I hated that he was vulnerable. It made me feel vulnerable for loving him.

But he told me if I was going to stay with him that I'd better back the fuck off.

It was one of the few times I'd heard James swear, so it made an impact. And became my mantra:

Back the fuck off, Santella.

Sometimes I'd have to remind myself. Like right now, when it took him ten minutes to get into his wheelchair. I stood on the sidewalk trying not to seem impatient and wishing I had a cigarette.

I'm pretty sure James knew that I snuck up to the roof to smoke every once in a while, because God knows I had to smell like an ashtray when I crawled back into bed, but he never said anything.

It was my one vice. I know that James was the one who'd lost the ability to walk, but it wasn't a cakewalk for me, either. The adjustment was stressful.

Django was the only witness to my night-time weakness on the rooftop terrace. And he didn't mind. He just sat at my feet and wagged his tail if I scratched behind his ears. Besides, I only snuck one on weekends. Otherwise it would interfere with my weekday workout in the morning.

Now, as James whipped his wheelchair in an expert spin 180 degrees to face me, a red-faced young man with a few beers under his belt stumbled out of the restaurant door and smacked into me. He practically knocked me over, and I whirled ready to swear at him but felt James's hand on my arm.

"Let's go, Gia."

I sighed. "Fine."

James was the only one in my life who'd ever managed to keep me on an even keel and instantly defuse my heated emotions. I smiled and squeezed his hand.

"I can smell the tortilla chips from here," I said.

———

Later, after stuffing ourselves with shrimp tacos and fresh, warm, crispy chips dipped in salsa and guacamole, we were happy and full and ready to get naked together. We headed out onto the sidewalk with me holding the door as James navigated the small step in his wheelchair. He cupped my ass with his palm, and I smacked his hand away. "Later, Romeo."

He laughed. He was playful and flirtatious after downing three beers. I'd skipped the booze. I'd been trying to cut back on my drinking. It made me slow and heavy-headed during my 5:00 a.m. Budo training.

The sun had set as we made our way toward the Jeep. Once we got there, I started toward the car to open the door for James but then stopped.

Back the fuck off, Santella. Let him do it on his own.

I was staring at my phone, trying to act like I wasn't watching him struggle to lift himself up into the seat, so I didn't notice the woman standing in the shadows of the store awning until she clutched at my sleeve.

"*Mija. Por favor.* My girl. She will die if they take her. Please take her. Please save her."

The woman, wearing a ripped and filthy floral shirt, looked around, her eyes wild. She had dark bags under her eyes and a slight harelip. She froze, eyes trained on something behind me. A look of sheer terror appeared across her face. It was the word "save" that stopped me in my tracks.

I turned to see what she was looking at, what had struck such fear in her. At first I didn't see them. The sidewalk was filled with pedestrians enjoying the warm night laughing and talking. People spoke Spanish and English and French, pushing baby strollers or holding hands. The only person who stood out at first was a man standing in front of the *carniceria*.

At first I thought she was looking at him. He stood still in the middle of the sidewalk staring at us. He was slight of frame—wiry—and wearing worn jeans and cowboy boots. But then I saw what must have frightened her—not far away from him two men stood side-by-side, eyes staring me down. Large white letters—POLICE and ICE—were emblazoned across their bulletproof vests.

"*Me puedes ayudar?*" Will you help me?

The woman thrust a little girl in a pink dress toward me. Before I could react, the woman turned and ran.

"Wait!" I yelled and started after her right as a crowd of people poured out of a nearby bar arm-in-arm and singing. I couldn't get past the rowdy throng on the crowded sidewalk.

"Stop! Come back!" I yelled, standing on tiptoe to look for the woman's dark head, but she'd already disappeared into the night.

I turned back. James met my eyes. His were wide and then he glanced over at the girl. She stood immobile next to my Jeep, her thin body shaking, holding a ripped and dirty plastic bag in front of her. Her eyes trained on something behind me.

BORDER LINE CHAPTER 2

I turned, looking in the direction the girl was facing.

The ICE agents were now running, coming straight toward us.

With one last glance toward where the woman had fled, I popped open the back door of the Jeep, lifted the girl, and plunked her into the seat, locking and slamming the door.

I was just about to open the driver's door when the two ICE agents arrived at the Jeep. One pounded on the passenger side window where James stared back coolly. The ICE agent was young and attractive but looked mean. He had dark hair, heavy eyebrows, and thick lips. The other man rounded the Jeep just as I slipped inside, slammed the door, and locked it. He glared at me and held up his badge. He was also handsome and baby-faced. He had fair skin, and his reddish hair was cut close to the scalp.

"Open up."

I cracked the window.

"Is there a problem?" I asked.

I saw his eyes dart toward the back seat. I was grateful that, even though it was illegal, I'd outfitted the Jeep with the darkest tinted windows you could buy. The man could barely see me. I hoped he couldn't see the girl cowering in the back seat.

"Can I see your identification?"

"Who are you?"

He held up an identification card. Samuel J. Miller. Immigrations and Customs Enforcement.

I was about to reply when James leaned over and slapped his own badge against the window. "San Francisco P.D. Is there a problem here?"

The agent actually stepped back a few inches.

James held the badge there for a second—a badge I didn't realize he still had—and then removed it.

"We were just about to make contact with a subject we believe is in the country illegally." He cleared his throat after he spoke. His Adam's apple bobbed. He was nervous.

"What does that have to do with us?" I said.

"We believe the subject's child is in the back seat of your vehicle. Could you please step out and speak to us?"

My heart raced up to my throat. *Think fast, Santella.*

"I don't understand."

"We saw you put a child in the back seat of this vehicle."

"Yes?"

"We believe she is the child of the illegal subject."

I laughed.

"Do you mean my daughter?"

"Pardon?"

"Are you referring to our daughter?"

"If we could just speak to the girl."

The other man, standing on the sidewalk near the passenger side window, glowered.

"Who's your partner?" I said.

He heard me and held his badge up to the window—Gabriel Hernandez. Immigrations and Customs Enforcement.

"Please remove the child from your vehicle so we can speak to her."

I waited to make sure my point got across crystal clearly. I bit the words out slowly: "No fucking way."

I raised an eyebrow and waited for them to argue. When they didn't, I said. "I will not have you traumatize my child because of your stupidity." I turned to James. "Do they have any legal right to speak to Maggie?"

I had no idea where that name sprang from but James didn't react.

"Nope." James folded his arms across his chest. I loved how he was right in step with me.

I heard a small sound from the back seat and hoped the girl wouldn't sit up and volunteer that Maggie was not, in fact, her name and that I was not her mother.

But the kid was sharp.

"Mama? What's going on?" her little voice piped up from the back seat.

Oh, my god. She was playing along, and she spoke English. With a thick-as-fuck accent, but still.

The young man's forehead crinkled.

"Excuse me, but we're already running late," I said. "Step away from the vehicle. I'd hate to accidentally run over your foot." I gave a wide, bright smile and started the car. Luckily, the space in front of me was empty, so I had a straight shot to pull back onto the road.

Before he could respond, I put my foot on the gas and slid into traffic. I eyed my rearview mirror, watching the two men standing in the street, eyes trained on my vehicle. I saw one of them take out a cell phone and make a call. It wasn't over yet.

I drove, heart racing and eyes flickering to my rearview mirror for about three blocks and then pulled down a side street where I parked.

I yanked off my seat belt and turned toward the back seat.

"*Come te llama?*" I asked.

"I speak English. My name is Rosalie."

"Rosalie, we are going to find you mother and get you back to her, okay?"

A look of confusion spread across her face, and I wondered how much English she really understood. But her next words stopped me.

"She says for me to live with you and James."

All the moisture disappeared from my mouth, and it felt like something was stuck in my throat. I tried to speak, but nothing came out at first.

Finally, I sputtered, "What the—" *fuck*? I bit the curse off right before it spilled out. "How do you know his name?"

James was now completely turned around. He seemed calmer than I was. Surprise, surprise. "Do I know your mother?" he asked.

The girl shook her head, her black braids swinging.

"Then how does she know me?"

I was starting to hyperventilate.

The girl shrugged. "*No se.* I mean, I don't know."

Her eyes grew wide, and she was full-on crying now. She stayed silent as a stream of tears poured out.

I needed to get my shit together. We were scaring this kid. I took a few deep breaths to calm myself and then tried again.

"Let's start from the top," I said, lowering my voice and making it as soothing as I could. "Okay, Rosalie. Did you say you were told to live with me and him?" I gestured toward James to make sure there was zero chance of confusion.

She nodded, her chin nearly touching her chest.

"Maybe I need to back up. What happened when you first came into America?"

"The men in ICE came and put us in their truck. But then

there was a car crash. The coyote hit their car. He helped us escape."

"Do you mean the car hit a coyote and crashed?"

"*No, el coyote.* He took us from our home. The whole way. And then he crashed a car to help us get away from the border patrol, but then he tried to take me and Miguel fought him. We ran, but he took Miguel."

"Who is Miguel?"

"*Mi hermano.* My brother."

"The coyote tried to take you?"

"*Si.* I mean yes."

I exhaled heavily. "Okay. What's the coyote's name?"

"They never tell. We pay them. My *abuela*, grandmother, in Guatemala, paid. To take us to America. Because what happened."

She looked down.

"What happened?"

She swallowed. "They came to our house and killed everybody—my aunt, *mi tia*, and killed my papa and my *tios*, my uncles."

I sat back in shock. "Where were you?"

"Under the bed. They beat up my *abuela*. She said she played dead."

"Where was your mama when all this happened?"

The girl paused and looked off in the distance for a few seconds.

"Where was your mother?"

"I don't know."

For some reason, I got the feeling she was lying. But I wasn't sure about which part.

"Oh, Rosalie. I'm so very, very sorry."

I'd heard of the atrocities in countries like Guatemala—the rapes and murders of entire families. It was why so many people from Central America were seeking asylum in America.

"What happened then?"

"We ran to the road. A woman in black made us get in her car." She frowned as if trying to remember. "She took us to a store. She made us get in a car with another woman. With blonde hair. She took us here and then we found you."

It sounded really convoluted and possibly even fabricated, but the girl's face was scrunched up in earnest as she told her story so I believed her.

"How did the blonde woman know where to find us?"

"The telephone. The woman in black called and told her."

I thought about that. The woman in black could only be one person. Eva. My aunt. I shook it off for a second. I'd come back to her.

"So, the woman in black told you to find me?"

"*Si*. She said I would know you for sure because of the scar."

My hand self-consciously raised to the long scar that ran from my cheekbone up to my hairline. King's mark on me.

"How old are you?"

"Seven."

"Can you tell me what the woman in black looked like?"

The girl looked off as if remembering. "*Bonita*. Pretty." The girl squinted. "Maybe like you? Your mother?"

"*Mi tia*." My aunt.

The girl nodded.

"Eva?" James frowned. "You mean the queen—"

"Okay then." I cut him off before he said it. *The Queen of Spades.*

"Your aunt is a queen?" The girl didn't miss a beat.

I laughed. "No. It's just a nickname."

"Oh." Rosalie's face fell.

In Sicily, finding a Jack of Spades on your doorstep was a

message from the mafia to mind your own business. If you found the Queen of Spades, you were marked for death.

Eva had taken on her moniker, The Queen of Spades, when she adopted the mafia tradition of leaving a playing card—the Queen of Spades—to warn her victims she was coming after them. She often killed them without warning and then left the card on the dead body. It was, literally, her calling card.

In Sicily, where my parents were from, Eva was a legend. She was a female Robin Hood, taking from—okay, let's face it, *murdering*—the rich and giving to the poor. When she was young, she took on all the mafia bosses single-handedly. I didn't know her entire story, but I knew she also kept close tabs on me and what was going on in my life, so I wasn't completely surprised to hear she was in Southern California, enacting her own brand of justice. But I was surprised she sent this girl to me.

I was about to question Rosalie even more when I saw a squad car pull onto the far end of the street.

James saw it too. "Let's get out of here in case they ask questions about a guy flashing a fake cop badge."

I gunned the motor, keeping an eye on the police car in my rearview mirror. "Fake?"

"It's not fake, I guess. It's just expired."

"Expired?" I was being a pest, I knew it. "I never knew you had that. And that you carry it around." I wondered if he'd whipped it out before. "Don't they take it away to prevent things just like that from happening?"

"Like what?"

If he was going to be difficult I was going to spell it out. Fine.

"Like people who are not working as cops using a police badge to get their way?"

"They felt sorry for me. Let me keep it." His voice had grown quiet.

I supposed when members of a police force shoot and paralyze a fellow officer based on orders from a corrupt cop, you might find one or two upstanding cops still in the department trying to do the right thing.

Reaching over, I squeezed his hand, but he gently pulled it away and turned to me with a smile. No pity allowed. Ever.

"Besides," he said. "It's come in handy in my new business."

"Impersonating a police officer? Oh no, James." That's when I noticed that a black sedan that had been behind me in the Mission district, was still behind me now that I was entering the Castro.

He smirked. "Wow, haven't things changed?"

I glared at him.

It wasn't so long ago that I was convinced we would never work out as a couple because he was such a goody-two-shoes cop, and I was a law breaker. Actually, way worse than a law-breaker. Because of me there were a few bodies "swimming with the fishes" as my Mafioso friends would say. But every death at my hands was justified. I'd swear that on my mother's grave.

But James was right. Now I was the one worried about the law. I turned left. The black car followed, about four cars behind.

"Fine," I said. "Just don't get caught."

"I don't intend to."

I made a sudden left turn.

"Jesus," James said, gripping the armrest.

"Hang tight. We might have a tail."

The tires squealed as I whipped a hard-right hand turn. I sped down the alley and made another right and then another back onto the first street. I was hoping to end up behind the black car. And I did.

It was slowing and made the first right I'd taken. I sped up and made the right turn down the alley, but didn't see the black car. I floored it.

"What the...?" James said. I came to a screeching halt where the alley met the next road and looked both ways. The black car was gone.

"Damn."

"Gia!"

"We lost them!" I shook my head.

"Wasn't that the point?"

"No."

That's when I caught sight of the girl's eyes in my rearview mirror. She was terrified.

I pulled over to the side of the road and half-turned in my seat.

"I'm so sorry. Did that scare you? My driving? I know it was a little crazy."

"Are they gone?"

That's when realization struck me. She wasn't afraid of how I was driving. She was scared of whomever was after her.

"We need to get you back to your mother. Did she say where she was going?"

"*Sí.*"

I whipped my head around. The one question I hadn't asked.

"Where?"

"*Autobús.*"

I yanked the steering wheel, made a U-turn, and headed for the bus station on Folsom Street. I slowed to a stop out front. I couldn't see a thing inside the terminal. The squat building was set back from the street and had corrugated steel siding. I was about to ask James to hop out and run inside but stopped myself in time. I grabbed his disabled placard from the center console, set it on the dash, flicked on my hazards, and jumped out.

"Be right back."

Inside, the station was nearly deserted. One guy was bundled up snoring in the corner surrounded by three large duffel bags. He was probably homeless and would get kicked out soon. In another corner, a family sat speaking what sounded like Korean, although my knowledge of the language was limited.

I headed toward the woman behind the counter who gave me a look with large hound dog eyes. Her light brown, curly hair was pulled back so tight I wondered if it gave her a headache.

"Hey," I said.

She raised an eyebrow. "May I help you?"

"Yeah. I'm looking for a friend. She was supposed to get on the bus tonight or tomorrow for L.A. or San Diego, if you go that far, but she forgot something."

"We go that far."

"You do? Cool." I stared at her. She stared back. She wasn't giving an inch.

"I was hoping to catch her before she left. What are the times for those buses?"

"We got a 10 p.m. coming up, and that's it until tomorrow morning at nine."

"Cool. What time did your last bus leave?" I put my palm flat on the counter between us.

"Seven thirty."

There's no way the woman could've caught that one since I saw her around eight.

"Did a woman with dark hair and a floral shirt buy a ticket for the ten o'clock bus."

She stared at me.

I pushed my palm forward, sliding it on the counter and then lifting a few fingers to show the twenty underneath.

The woman didn't turn her head, but her eyes flickered from left to right. I noticed a security camera directly behind her. She picked up a piece of paper and put it over my hand. I removed my hand so the money stayed underneath the paper.

"I think that ten o'clock bus might be empty."

She slid the paper with the money underneath toward her.

"How can I find out if it leaves here empty? I'd really like to make sure this woman gets what she forgot. She'll be very sad to go home without it."

The woman yawned. "Ticket office closes at ten. Nobody can get a ticket after that."

"Okay. Thanks."

I glanced at my phone. It was nine.

"One more question. Is this the only place to wait for the bus?" I glanced around the room.

"'Less you want to wait outside, then yes."

"Okay. Thanks."

Before I walked outside, I poked my head in both the men's and women's bathrooms. They were empty.

I went back out to the Jeep and stopped at the passenger side. James rolled down the window and winked. "Hey, cutie."

I peeked in the back. Rosalie was staring right at me.

I sighed. I wasn't going to make them sit in the car with me for an hour. I'd get the mother and bring her back to the loft. The two of them could catch a bus in the morning.

"I think I'm going to drop you guys off at home," I said. I looked at the girl. "I'll bring your mother there when I find her."

"Got it," James said.

The girl just stared at me.

I rounded the hood and hopped back in. Before I started the car, I turned to the back seat.

"Hey, Rosalie. We're going to have a sleepover at my house tonight. I can't wait to introduce you to my dog. He's a big lug. Very sweet though. His name is Django."

"*Perro?*"

"*Si.* He's a good dog. He likes little girls." As soon as I said the words I hoped I wasn't lying. I guess we'd soon find out.

As we pulled away I saw a black car pull up in front of the

bus station. As I watched in my rearview mirror, my heart-raced to see one of the ICE agents hop out and walk toward the station's front door.

Close call.

Are you loving *Border Line*? Scan the QR code below to order your copy today!

ALSO BY KRISTI BELCAMINO

Enjoying Kristi Belcamino? Scan the code below to see her Amazon Author page!

Gia Santella Crime Thriller Series

Vendetta

Vigilante

Vengeance

Black Widow

Day of the Dead

Border Line

Night Fall

Stone Cold

Cold as Death

Cold Blooded

Dark Shadows

Dark Vengeance

Dark Justice

Deadly Justice

Deadly Lies

Additional books in series:

Taste of Vengeance

Lone Raven

Vigilante Crime Series

Blood & Roses

Blood & Fire

Blood & Bone

Blood & Tears

Queen of Spades Thrillers

Queen of Spades

The One-Eyed Jack

The Suicide King

The Ace of Clubs

The Joker

The Wild Card

High Stakes

Poker Face

Standalone Novels

Coming For You

Sanctuary City

The Girl in the River

Buried Secrets

Dead Wrong (Young Adult Mystery)

Gabriella Giovanni Mystery Series

Blessed are the Dead

Blessed are the Meek

Blessed are Those Who Weep

Blessed are Those Who Mourn

Blessed are the Peacemakers

Blessed are the Merciful

Nonfiction

Letters from a Serial Killer

ALSO BY WITHOUT WARRANT

More Thriller Series from Without Warrant Authors

Dana Gray Mysteries by C.J. Cross

Girl Left Behind

Girl on the Hill

Girl in the Grave

The Kenzie Gilmore Series by Biba Pearce

Afterburn

Dead Heat

Heatwave

Burnout

Deep Heat

Fever Pitch

Storm Surge (Coming Soon)

Willow Grace FBI Thrillers by Anya Mora

Shadow of Grace

Condition of Grace (Coming Soon)

Gia Santella Crime Thriller Series

by Kristi Belcamino

Vendetta

Vigilante

Vengeance

Black Widow

Day of the Dead

Border Line

Night Fall

Stone Cold

Cold as Death

Cold Blooded

Dark Shadows

Dark Vengeance

Dark Justice

Deadly Justice

Deadly Lies

Vigilante Crime Series by Kristi Belcamino

Blood & Roses

Blood & Fire

Blood & Bone

Blood & Tears

Queen of Spades Thrillers by Kristi Belcamino

Queen of Spades

The One-Eyed Jack

The Suicide King

The Ace of Clubs

The Joker

The Wild Card

High Stakes

Poker Face

AUTHOR'S NOTE

When I was 16, I read Jackie Collins' book, *Lucky*, and it rocked my world. For the first time in my prolific reading life (yes, I was the kid holed up in my room reading as many books as I could as often as I could), I met a character who was not only Italian-American like me, but a strong, powerful, and successful badass woman who didn't take crap from anybody and loved to have sex!

Although I had dreamed of being a writer, it never seemed like a realistic dream and my attempts at writing seemed pitiful. So I studied journalism and became a reporter—it was a way to be a writer and have a steady paycheck.

It was only when I was in my forties that I got the guts to write a book. And it was a few years after that I was brave enough to write the character I really wanted to write—Gia Santella.

She's not Lucky Santangelo, of course. I mean, nobody could be as cool as Lucky is, but I like to think that maybe Gia and Lucky would have been friends.

Gia is my alter ego. The woman who does and says things I

never could or would, but whom I admire and would love to be friends with.

If you like her, I'm pretty sure we'd be the best of friends in real life!

x Kristi

ABOUT THE AUTHOR

Kristi Belcamino is a USA Today bestseller, an Agatha, Anthony, Barry & Macavity finalist, and an Italian Mama who bakes a tasty biscotti.

Her books feature strong, kickass, independent women facing unspeakable evil in order to seek justice for those unable to do so themselves.

In her former life, as an award-winning crime reporter at newspapers in California, she flew over Big Sur in an FA-18 jet with the Blue Angels, raced a Dodge Viper at Laguna Seca, attended barbecues at the morgue, and conversed with serial killers.

During her decade covering crime, Belcamino wrote and reported about many high-profile cases including the Laci Peterson murder and Chandra Levy disappearance. She has appeared on *Inside Edition* and local television shows. She now writes fiction and works part-time as a reporter covering the police beat for the St. Paul *Pioneer Press*.

Her work has appeared in such prominent publications as *Salon*, the *Miami Herald*, *San Jose Mercury News,* and *Chicago Tribune*.

facebook.com/kristibelcaminobooks

instagram.com/kristibelcaminobooks

tiktok.com/@kristibelcaminobooks